# W.C. HOLLOWAY

*"America's New Storyteller"*

GOOD 2 GO PUBLISHING

**Love & Deception**
Written by W.C. Holloway
Cover Design: Davida Baldwin – Odd Ball Designs
Typesetter: Mychea
ISBN: 9781947340435

Published 2019 by Good2Go Publishing
7311 W. Glass Lane • Laveen, AZ 85339
www.good2gopublishing.com
https://twitter.com/good2gobooks
G2G@good2gopublishing.com
www.facebook.com/good2gopublishing
www.instagram.com/good2gopublishing

## DEDICATION

*For my big sister Diane Holloway, you'll never be forgotten.*

## PROLOGUE

Love is one of the world's most intricate mysteries: a long-standing emotion with an infinite history. No one can evade it, even if you love to hate it. Some love the institution of the emotion and the comfort it brings—the euphoric sensation or a taste of pleasure, like apple pie with ice cream. It is a fantasy fulfilled and the completion of a dream.

Love is someone who appreciates you for all your worth. One who without hesitation caters to your needs and desires, giving you what you deserve.

Love embraces all things you don't like about yourself. It opens your eyes to a world of emotional wealth.

Love is patient, yet understanding. It weathers the storms, dark times, or sad or bad times; but when it's good, it feels good, even though it's demanding.

Love is about trust, respect, and honoring the one you're with. It's about communication and building a bond of happiness with no expiration.

But, love in the wrong hands can lead to visual and emotional deception. Nothing is what you picture it to be.

# CHAPTER 1

***Present day: Forest Hills Estates; Harrisburg, Pennsylvania***

"This area is so beautiful, and the house is big enough to settle in and start a family one day," Sarah Duvall said, speaking to her movers as they unloaded her furniture and took it into her new home on a cul de sac in Forest Hills Estates. This was a well-to-do neighborhood that boasted four and five thousand-square-foot homes.

Sarah found herself in the Harrisburg suburbs on a career move from Charleston, South Carolina. The southern belle didn't mind the move since she was single. It allowed her to bury some of her past by leaving it all behind her.

The five foot five, 142-pound redhead was a country girl at heart with big-city dreams and aspirations. She always kept the words of her father in mind: Never give in. Never give up on your dreams or things you love to do. These were words she would never forget, since it was her way of keeping him alive after him being gone two years now. But he left her with two thousand acres since she was the only child. She sold that land for well over $3 million, which allowed her to afford her new home.

Sarah stood alongside the moving truck and directed her movers as to where she wanted things to go.

"Now you better be careful with that. My daddy gave me that," she said, referring to a hand-carved cherry wood bench with her name engraved on it along with the words Daddy's Angel.

Her womanly instincts made her look over her shoulder as a feeling came over her as if she was being watched. She was. Two houses to the right of hers stood a man on his porch with his newspaper in one hand and a bottle of Gatorade in the other.

She didn't pay those items any mind. What she did notice was the tank top he was wearing that showed off his fit body and tight muscles that glistened from sweat.

"Aye! Aye, you!" Sarah yelled out while waving to him with her priceless commercial smile with innocent dimples that gave her smile a warm and welcoming appeal.

He stood there and looked on at her as he tilted his Gatorade to refuel.

"Oh my Lord, look at this!" she voiced to herself looking at his arms. "You can come over and help with them big ole arms," she yelled out with a smile.

The look on his face was one of confusion since he just worked out and could feel the burn. He was not about to volunteer his services, plus he thought she was crazy with all the yelling and waving.

"You want me?" he said, pointing to himself with the newspaper.

"Big arms, good looking, and no brains!" she said in a low tone to herself while still smiling. "Well, I don't see anyone else standing there looking like they can curl a Volkswagen," she said, making him laugh before turning to shut his front door and make his way over to her.

As he was approaching, he started taking in all of her natural beauty: radiant red hair, glowing hazel-green eyes, seductive pink lips, and an overall natural look. She wore blue short shorts with a white T-shirt boasting the words Beautiful, Country & Blessed in big red letters outlined with silver glitter that matched her silver-and-red Nike Air Max sneakers. He appreciated all that he saw in his new neighbor. He was just hoping she was a little more quiet than her introduction indicated.

"I take it you didn't want to wait on me to welcome you to the neighborhood?" he said with a smile after extending his hand to shake hers.

She was so focused on his pumped arms and now up-close massive chest, that she briefly became lost in the moment of his brown skin being her playground.

"Oh, oh my, I'm sorry," she said while shaking

his hand. "You still can welcome me by showing your hospitality and using those big muscles to help get my things inside."

She batted her eyes and worked her Southern charm.

"I get it. You think you can come here to my neighborhood and direct me to move your things without even formally introducing yourself or asking me my name?" he responded lightly to amuse her and have fun with the situation.

"Well excuse my manners, and forgive me for being so rude," she responded, caught off guard. Yet her eyes still visually crawled all over his body up until she locked eyes with him. "I'm Sarah Duvall from Charleston, South Carolina. I'm very single and independent. Not that I don't need a man, just ain't found one worth welcoming into my heart and life."

"Well, Ms. Duvall."

"Please, call me Sarah," she said, placing her soft hand on his bicep.

It was not thought out or planned, it just happened. Jesus.

*Did I just put my hand on him?* she questioned herself inside while smiling on the outside as she looked into his eyes.

*Friendly and hands-on?* he thought to himself.

"My name is Travon, but my friends call me

Trae."

Travon stood six foot two and weighed a fit 225 pounds from exercising and weight training. He also kept a strict no red meat diet that allowed him to have the results he did.

Travon's mother was Italian American and his father African American, which gave him the best of both worlds. He had a light brown skin tone, grayish-colored eyes, and pretty-boy black silky hair with waves all the way around on his close haircut. Everything flowed with his baby face, and he looked younger than his actual age of twenty-six.

"You know what, Trae? I can call you Trae, right?" she said, being funny.

"If you plan on being my friend; as I stated, only my friends call me Trae," he responded.

"Well, Travon," she said, not wanting to be in any friend zone, so to speak, especially with the brief images of all the fun she was having with his body. "Tell me about yourself and who's keeping you company."

"Normally people go out on dates and talk about these things first, but I take it that where you're from down South, it's a little different?"

"No, no, I just like to cut straight to it, you know, with me being the honest type. I like to get the same in return."

He took a moment to look away from her luring glowing green eyes that seemed to pull him in the more they spoke. As strange as it was, she too started feeling the same way while looking into his glassy gray eyes. Could this be chemistry? They both allowed the thought to enter their mind; however, they didn't want to rush what was meant to be anyway. She didn't want to resist what was natural. On the other hand, he tried to evade it by looking at his white G-Shock watch.

"Somewhere to be?" she questioned, not wanting him to leave just yet, especially as she was trying to get to know him.

"Yes, but I'll make it up to you tonight and formally welcome you to this neighborhood. I'll even cook dinner, and you can ask me as many questions as you desire. By the way, Sarah, I don't cook for just anyone, especially strangers," he said while walking away trying to be funny.

"I'm not a stranger now. You know my first and last name as well as where I live. Besides, if I like your cooking, then dessert will be my treat to you."

Right then his mind started racing with sexual thoughts, especially after seeing her eyes sparkle followed by her salaciously biting her bottom lip. He was officially caught in her whirlwind. This player had never seen her kind before. Now he was in for a long ride.

"Is 6:00 p.m. fine with you?" he asked.

"Yes it is. Oh, and just so you know, I don't eat red meat," she said still smiling. He, too, smiled and appreciated that her diet mirrored his. He stopped in mid-stride.

"Any other requests?" he asked, with an *I can't wait until tonight* look in his eyes.

"Just be a gentleman, and you'll always get what you deserve."

*Damn. Did she really just say that?* he thought.

"I would not be anything else," he said with a wave before entering his home and leaving her with the thoughts of how tonight was going to be.

She wanted to know more about him. There was something that was intriguing about him, and not just physical attraction, which is what most women would say about him. This was different. But only time would tell her all she needed to know.

## Chapter 2

Sarah was settling into her new place and trying to make her house a home. Being single forced her to be independent. Also, her father told her growing up that she didn't have to depend on a man. He explained in the end of his demise when he left her financially stable. So the only thing a man could bring to the table was himself emotionally, physically, and mentally—the raw body of a relationship that could bring about love.

On the other hand, her mother, Candice, had stopped speaking to her for now due to the career decisions she had made. Sarah had a few friends at her workplace that seemed distant at times. Other than that, she didn't mind her alone time. She took a break from moving all of her things around and sat on the bench that her father had made for her. She then took a drink from her 64-ounce Big Gulp she grabbed at the 7-11 mini-mart.

The movers were all gone over an hour now, leaving her to get the little things in order. As she was taking a sip, she started thinking about her new life and new beginning. She was now on a new path to fulfill her destiny and goals. It was almost like finding the pieces to the puzzle she had been working on for years.

In the midst of these thoughts, bringing her back to the living room and moment, her doorbell sounded. Travon entered her mind and put a smile on her face as she placed her soda down before pulling her hair back to display her facial features, natural beauty, and sleek jaw line even more. Since she was in the house, she no longer wore her sneakers. She was barefoot in the comfort of the new home.

She came to the dual doors with the oval-shaped stained glass and looked through it. An older woman was on the other side that looked to be in her late forties or early fifties.

"Hello, how are you doing?"

"Well, I'm just fine. Trying to settle in here," Sarah said with her Southern accent permeating.

"I'm Connie Peterson. I live in the third house to the left of you. The other women would usually be here to welcome you into the neighborhood, but they're all out of town. So I came with flowers and pamphlets on how we conduct ourselves here in Forest Hills Estates," Connie said, sounding a little snobby, yet with a smile trying to bring ease and displaying a welcoming sign.

Connie only stood five foot one and had blonde hair that was clearly dyed from its graying or signs of aging. She also had a noticeable nose and lip job, along with work around the eyes to rid her of the crow's feet. One thing most people overlook is the neck and hands, which seem to tell the age.

Sarah didn't care too much about the rules, especially since she paid in the high six figures to reside here.

"Well, thank you for the flowers, and I'll be sure to look over this book thing here, because I would not want to offend anyone with my Southern etiquette," Sarah said with her Southern accent filled with sarcasm.

"If I can help you settle in or feel more welcome, just ask," Connie responded.

Travon entered her mind again, and she wondered if this woman could give her some insight on who he really was. Her eyes shifted toward his house as those thoughts entered her mind.

"What's Travon's story?" she asked, still looking toward his place. Connie also glanced over briefly before speaking.

"He's very handsome and respectful. Basically, a mystery that intrigues even those ladies who are married," Connie emphasized, showing off her three-carat diamond engagement ring that interlocked with her diamond-encrusted wedding band.

"Is he single?"

"I'm surprised you didn't ask him when you yelled him over to you earlier," Connie said, which made Sarah realize she was the nosey neighbor type. "He's whatever you want him to be, or whatever you believe he is. Like I said, he's a mystery."

Sarah could not wait until diner to see what he was all about. The physical attraction was evident, but what else was he capable of bringing to the table, and was it what she was looking for? Sarah's mind all but came to a halt with the thoughts she was having of tonight's dinner when she noticed a candy-apple-red Porsche Panamera pull up to his home, which got both her and Connie's attention.

"Cute car!" Sarah said. "Mmmh!" she added, after seeing the car come to a halt and blow the horn. What really caught Sarah's attention was the female driver. "Who's the lady friend?"

"It sounds to me like you really have your eyes set out for this one. Don't get yourself caught up. As for the female—" Connie paused, after taking a look to see if she recognized the face—"I don't know her name, but the face I've seen around before."

"So he's a player and that's his girl?" Sarah asked after having second thoughts about tonight's dinner.

"I would not say she is his girlfriend, since she has never stepped foot inside his home. She pulls up, waits on him to come out, and that's as far as I know. Like I said, he is a mystery."

As those words flowed from Connie's mouth, the Latina in the driver's seat turned and made eye contact with Sarah. Both women locked eyes on one another as if they had seen one another before. But they could not quite put their finger on it just yet. However, their female intuition alerted them both.

Travon exited his home in a light-blue linen two-piece with tan suede Gucci shoes and a Ulysse Nardin watch, the Sonata streamline with titanium case and ceramic bezel. He wore no other jewelry. He didn't look flashy, however, only smooth, confident, and appealing to the eyes of Connie and Sarah.

"He would be my best kept secret only if he knew how much I appreciated seeing him," Connie said, placing her hand across her chest and feeling her heart pick up its beat.

"He would also be the reason you ended up divorced," Sarah said, reminding her that she was married.

She also wanted Connie to keep her distance, so as a single woman, she could have her proper chance with him.

Travon turned to see the women and gave them both a smile as he waved. Each of them lit up inside and out.

"You look good in baby blue!" Sarah spewed out.

She could not help herself; besides, she wanted to stick out to him. He embraced the compliment and acknowledged her with a nod before slipping into the car. The Latina drove off, leaving the two desperate-looking housewives drooling. Sarah stood there in her own world of seduction with Travon, when Connie waved her hand in front of her face.

"Hello, come back now. Don't lose yourself!" Connie said upon seeing Sarah with her arms folded under her breasts. She had her right hand and finger resting on her lips and chased after the image she was having. A smile formed when she remembered that she would see him tonight.

"A mystery he is, and it burns me with desire to want to know more about him," Sarah said in a Southern drawl that always seemed to be filled with a hint of sarcasm. "Well, Connie, I guess I'll be going now. I have some things I need to tend to."

"I'll see you later, young lady. Be careful chasing after the rabbit's tail," she said as she walked away and left Sarah with that thought.

## Chapter 3

"I see you have a new neighbor, papi?" Rosanna said to Travon as she drove off.

Rosanna was Dominican born, stood five foot six, and filled out every curve of her body, only weighing 120 pounds of toned perfection. She had long silky black hair that touched the middle of her back, honey-brown eyes, and a luring smile with a mole above the left side of her lip that added to her smile of intrigue.

Rosanna was Travon's trusted driver and assistant, and she handled his day-to-day affairs, which allowed her to become aware of all of his surroundings.

"Is this a personal or business question?" he asked after hearing the tone in her voice.

On more than one occasion, Rosanna and Travon shared intimate space, even though it was a rule of his not to cross work and personal lines. But it happened and they enjoyed it. In fact, they loved it and each other, but they agreed—while it was still good—to keep it good and become friends and co-workers, and as well to maintain their unique bond.

"You don't have to be on the defensive all the time. I was just asking because she was all in my face."

"Maybe she recognizes you from somewhere?"

Rosanna gave him a look that was filled with question and confusion.

"How do you think she would know me, estupido? I barely know myself with all that has been going on in the last five years."

"Pull over, please," he requested after hearing her voice break backed by emotions she still might have for him.

He thought that something maybe eating at her as if she was living two lives or too many lies. She did as he requested and pulled the car over. He placed his hand on her leg. His touch always gave her the comfort she yearned for and missed from him.

"Are you okay?"

She nodded her head, and he reached up and wiped away a tear in the corner of her eye.

"Are we good? Is everything with us still good?"

She nodded again, this time turning to look into his eyes.

"Everything is good, papi," she said before shifting back to the business mind-set. "You have a meeting scheduled with the California investors. After that, you have a meeting at the club to ensure they're in line with this weekend's celebrity guest DJ Khalid hosting the CÎROC Bash. You're scheduled time with Jamir at 4:00. If you like, I can extend the meeting time and close out the day?"

"That isn't necessary. I have a six o'clock dinner arrangement at the house," he responded, keeping Sarah in mind.

"The house?" she questioned.

He nodded as she held back the personal question she had behind it.

"Okay, I'll schedule that in."

"Yes."

"Yes what?"

"I did meet my neighbor after my morning workout. She wanted me to help her movers with her things. I declined."

"It's not sounding like it. She must be crazy to even ask you that, but go on."

"That's what I was thinking when she asked me to help. However, that led to a conversation that evolved into dinner tonight."

"Really, so you're inviting a stranger to the house?"

"I said that to her, but she made it clear that I know her full name and address, so I bought into it; besides, you know I'm a people pleaser at times. If I can make everyone in the world smile just once, then I serve my purpose and my legacy will live on."

Rosanna rolled her eyes at his words. She mashed the gas, which jarred him and caught him off guard, pushing him back into his seat.

"I think you may have a few investors from Miami coming into town to look at a few properties within a day or so. Maybe you can sell the house. I think it's time for a change," she said, still sounding like her words were backed by emotions and sarcasm.

Travon was smart and had the best of both worlds. He had lived both a street life as well as a suburban life. Everyone has their fair share of good and bad. He attended Harrisburg Academy and graduated with distinguishing grades. He then went off to college, where he majored in business and marketing. In college, he also found himself networking and meeting different people who shared his same interests in life. He followed the money and made his mint in real estate, alongside his night clubs in Harrisburg, Philadelphia, Atlanta, and soon New York City.

"Change sounds good. Now slow down. I want to make it to this meeting alive."

Rosanna rambled on in Spanish about what she was thinking and feeling about what was going on with him and this new girl. Even though she said she was all right with it, she was not. There was something about him that made women gravitate toward him when he was pursuing them and when it was over. Rosanna also didn't trust the neighbor for some reason. It was her familiar-looking face that left bad thoughts in her mind.

"My pretty love, no one can replace you or the bond we have. We have history, and we also have a unique understanding."

His words alone brought a halt to her rambling. He comforted her inside and out, which placed a smile on her face. She was happy for now; however, he could feel that there was something far deeper bothering her. He had known her for over five years now, and both her behavior and attitude were telling. He just had to figure it out and let her express what was going on or let time run its course.

## Chapter 4

Travon was in his downtown high-rise office. His associates flew in from California to entertain the idea of investing in his business, the Global Image Group, which he had started with his two college buddies: Ricardo Sanchez and Byron Malory.

Normally, Ricardo handled all of the Los Angeles affairs with their office out there; however, he wanted to be present today to make sure the meeting with these investors went smoothly, since they were looking to expand their empire. Ricardo was a single Colombian-American that stood five foot eleven. He had a medium build, dark brown eyes, thick eyebrows, a clean-shaven face, and a strong jaw line. He was keen on all business and never lost focus when it was game time and time to handle business. However, in his down time, he enjoyed the ladies and trips to the casinos.

Byron stood six foot two and probably could have been a basketball player since he was so good in college, but his focus turned to chasing the title and lifestyle of being a mogul. Byron's baby-blue eyes seemed to glow with his golden tan from his recent vacation to Cancun. His close-shaven beard was shaped up with razor perfection and made him look like a Gucci model. But he was a serious businessman and a dedicated husband to his beautiful wife, whom he met during his travels to Japan. They also had two children, a boy and a girl. Most people thought he had the perfect family. Although he was doing well at only twenty-eight years old, he wanted more financial success.

Ricardo had the idea of building casinos due to his love and passion for them, along with the women they would bring. On the other hand, Travon, didn't think it was a good idea to own a casino with a partner that could potentially hurt the business from both ends.

The two men were from California. One was an elderly gentleman originally from Mexico, and the other was Italian-American. Each looked the part of a multimillionaire, and they were backed by even more powerful people. Everyone sat at the oval-shaped table in the conference room and exchanged their views on business before getting to the point and core of it all.

Rosanna sat in a chair directly behind Travon, where she took notes and acted as the eyes and ears in the meeting. She would write down everything that she viewed as vital to the meeting as well as anything Travon asked her to jot down. Travon was very resourceful and always had a background check run on anyone and everyone with whom he did business or whom he invited into his circle, whether it be for business or pleasure.

He figured whoever a person brings around in their life could be the deciding point to one's success in any venture, whether it be financial or emotional.

"Mr. Guzman, my colleagues and I normally meet out in the field onsite where potential business is being conducted, which allows everyone's views to be tangible instead of having to verbally paint the picture. However, my associate, Ricardo, recommended this meeting for a reason," Travon began as he turned on his professional business mind-set.

Without question, Travon was the driving force among the three associates. Although, each one of them strongly represented the Global Image Group and other business ventures just as well.

Mr. Guzman was only five foot five with a medium build at 195 pounds. The Mexican-born businessman was driven to succeed by achieving the American dream with the hopes of one day becoming a citizen.

"Amigos, yo tengo chabo para ti. Tu necessito mi dinero o no?"

"Rosanna, tell Mr. Guzman that we prefer English, please," Travon said not knowing enough Spanish to hold a full conversation.

"Señor Guzman, nosotros necessito to habla Ingles, por favor," she said.

"Comprendidos, pero mi Ingles as mas o menos."

"Esta bien, señor."

"Señor Robinson," Mr. Guzman addressed Travon by his last name. "I come with the financial backing to build this resort that your friend mentioned."

"Whoa! Hold on a second, Mr. Guzman," Travon said while looking over at his partner. "Ricardo, you told me we were going with just a casino in and out, not a resort that extends to further insurances and liabilities as well as overhead."

Ricardo gave a look on his face that displayed that he was caught for failing to disclose this information to his partners. Travon had always stressed the need to be in the loop on any financial transactions made using the company's name.

"I sent this info to your assistants," Ricardo said, trying to bail himself out of it.

"Ladies, tell me he is wrong about this," Travon said, turning to his assistants, Rosanna and two other women she hired to help her.

"This e-mail came in just as the meeting started, sir," Jennifer, the young brunette, said sheepishly and slightly in fear of losing her job.

"Thank you, Jennifer," Travon said after nodding to her and then turning to his partner.

"Nice try, Ricardo. It is not what we do, but you gave it an effort," he said before focusing back to the meeting. "Can everyone other than those sitting at this table step out for a moment, please?" Travon asked nicely, wanting to address everyone inside without everyone's assistants and lawyers present.

Everyone exited the room, leaving the California associates to speak in private with Travon and his partners. The lawyer, bodyguards, and assistants could see into the floor-to-ceiling glass conference room as they stood outside waiting to be waved back into the room.

Rosanna wanted to be present, because part of her worried about Travon. But her love for him had to be suppressed due to a mutual agreement they had together.

Rosanna's personal cell phone sounded off, which got her immediate attention as she shifted her eyes away from Travon inside the meeting room. Anonymous Caller appeared on her phone screen. She sent it to voicemail since she didn't want to take a blocked call.

Within thirty seconds the phone sounded off again. This time a text message came through. She accessed the message and it read: *How long do you think this can last? We need to talk!*

Reading the text made her heart jump in fear

because she felt as if her world and the walls around her would soon close in.

As she looked away from the text message, Travon glanced over at her and the others and tried to get their attention to come back into the room. He also noticed the look on her face, which he would address at a later time.

They all made their way back into the room, when Rosanna's cell phone rang again. As if she didn't hear it ringing, she gave Travon a brief smile. She wanted to assure him that everything was still good. She then sent the call to voicemail. However, the look that Travon gave her was noticed by his California associate, Carmine Delarossa.

Carmine was a real suave Italian guy that looked like a made man, with his black-and-silver hair combed back and clean-shaven face. He was well groomed in his gray, silk two-piece Giorgio Armani tailored suit. He was rich and flashy and wore a diamond-encrusted pinky ring that flowed with his diamond Bentley Bernato watch made by Breitling.

Carmine knew people from around the world. He was a silent investor in many of the world's notable destinations from Dubai to Brazil. He was also a keen individual when it came to business and knowing those around him as well as when things didn't seem as good as they appeared.

He had it set in his mind that he was going to do a full check on the Global Image Group and their assistants, since they were the closest to the three businessmen.

"Rosanna, you and or the other ladies can schedule another meeting a week from today that will take place in Las Vegas. With that said, have a nice day and flight back to California," Travon added.

"Te beo despues, amigos," Mr. Guzman said, nodding his head before exiting the room with Carmine and their associates.

## Chapter 5

As they were exiting the conference room, Travon pulled Rosanna to the side to see what was going on with her since she didn't seem like herself.

"Your phone has been keeping you distracted lately. Who's the new guy?"

"Is this a personal question you're asking me in a business environment?"

"A question with a question. Okay I deserve that," he said with a transient smile before a more firm look graced his face. "With these new investors comes a level of power and seriousness. I need to know we're good at all times, business and personal. Image is everything, and we are the Global Image Group."

"You focus on the big things, and I'll keep the rest in line," she responded, not wanting to continue this conversation.

Rosanna had a secret she needed to keep from him for now, because her love for him and mutual bond they had made this mentally and emotionally tortuous. She knew she needed to figure out what was going on and how she was going to resolve this without bringing harm to him or anyone else.

As they prepared to leave, she saw a familiar face heading toward the same elevator as her and Travon. The two of them were in a rush to get to the next meeting at the club with his employees.

The person she was looking at was someone from her past that Travon didn't know. It was someone she wanted and needed to keep a secret. Questions lingered inside her head:

*Why is he here, and why now?*

*Why is he not saying anything?*

*Is he the one that left the message and kept calling?*

Her heart beat a little faster when she saw that the man with the familiar face was holding the door to the elevator when he saw them coming. She didn't want to be close to him, let alone be closed in. She had to think of something.

*This is not going to work.*

*What if he exposes my truth and secret?*

Suddenly, an idea came to her. She dropped her things: phone, small handbag, and contracts that Travon would look at later between meetings.

"Ahi, Dios mio," she said as she squatted down to retrieve her things. "You can let the door go. We'll catch the next one," she said, not wanting to get into the elevator with him.

"Thank you anyway," Travon said politely as he knelt down to help his assistant.

Right then he could see how nervous she was with her hands shaking as if she had just seen a ghost or experienced some trauma.

Being precocious, having the mind-set of a chess wizard, and always thinking ahead, he started piecing it all together. She didn't have to say anything. Something terribly wrong was disturbing her.

"Too much caffeine this morning?" he asked while still looking at her shaking.

"Yes, I guess I put too much sugar in it, too," she replied after giving a vacuous smile through her nerves before standing to her feet with all of her things back in place.

"If you think you may drop these things again, I'll hold them for you until you pull yourself together," he said, trying to make her feel at ease so he could get the secret out of her that was eating her up inside.

He didn't feel a need to force it out of her. His way of doing things was to allow time to take its course. Besides, he had a busy schedule today, so this could wait.

Once in the elevator, there was silence unlike any other time. Silence for seven floors down to the ground floor. The silence allowed Travon to mentally assess what was going on with his go-to assistant, Rosanna. The silence somehow tormented her as her own thoughts and feelings overwhelmed her.

The bell chimed to signify that the elevator had

reached the ground floor. The doors parted open like a breath of fresh air. She took a noticeable deep breath before exiting. Travon was at her side as they made their way through the lobby area.

She saw the same man again. Instantly, fear swept over her again. She clenched her things that she was holding while her heart thumped against her chest. Her eyes locked onto him as he leaned against his car in front of the building. His arms were folded and he had a mischievous grin.

*This is the end of the good relationship and friendship I have with Travon*, she thought. *Whatever happens is meant to be.* She thought about conceding to the idea of being exposed. She briefly closed her eyes in mid-stride and thought that this situation could not be happening. She then opened her eyes and he was still there. He was opening the car door for a female who walked right passed her. She didn't recognize the female; in fact, she had never seen her before. *I wonder who she is?* Rosanna thought. *Maybe she works on another floor?* However, it didn't change the fact that the other familiar face was still present. She didn't view this as a coincidence.

Travon caught the smirk on the gentleman's face which raised his awareness until the female passed them by. He then understood what the smirk was all about, or so he thought.

"Excuse me, Ms. Santos," a voice came from the right side of Rosanna.

Rosanna turned toward the voice and saw that it was the receptionist getting her attention. She quickly made her way over to the counter.

"What's going on?" she asked the receptionist.

"I have a verbal message for you. He says to contact him before you find yourself in a deep bind. He said you're a good girl, so you'll figure it all out," the receptionist said.

Rosanna took a deep breath and tried to wrap her head around all of this. The familiar face and the message only confirmed that he was who she thought he was. She turned back around and joined Travon as if nothing had happened.

"Are you ready now?" he asked.

"I'm always ready," she fired back, wanting to shift his attention away from asking her what the receptionist wanted her for.

As they exited the building, she looked around for the familiar face, but he was gone. He was now nowhere in sight, or so she thought.

## Chapter 6

At 2:49 p.m., Travon and Rosanna arrived at the Red Scorpion nightclub, one of his clubs that had a gold scorpion lit with red lighting at the entrance and scorpion artwork throughout the club.

He entered the club and saw his staff busy stocking the bars and keeping things in line. The staff was completing day-to-day entertainment and preparing a special request for the guests.

The Red Scorpion was located a few blocks from the Harrisburg East Mall. It was the perfect location, with a large number of restaurants in the area; however, it was also its own attraction for those willing to experience the affluent nightclub life.

"Mr. Robinson, how's everything going today?"

"I'm going, and how are things going here today, Melissa?" he asked.

Melissa Christie was the twenty-two-year-old driven manager of the Red Scorpion. She stood five foot nine. She had model looks and was bi-racial, just like Travon. Her hazel-brown eyes sparkled as much as her smile did, with dimples of innocence that added to her charm. Melissa wore her hair cut short, which made her look like a young Halle Berry. She, too, had a thing for Travon and his smooth ways. However, she enjoyed her time with him whenever it was convenient to his overwhelming schedule. Their time together was always explosive when they became intimate. What made her stand out from the other women that crossed his path was that she thinks like a guy. She was in it for the good sex and was okay that he would go and do him. No strings attached. But she did accept gifts from him from time to time.

On the other hand, Rosanna was not aware of their secret rendezvous. Even his friends didn't know all of his female friends. He felt it was best that way. He figured that emotions could destroy a business if it ever became personal.

"In case you're wondering about the CÎROC Bash, we have all we need. Everything is in order. The reservations are booked for the suites we have overlooking the dance floor. The floor suites are also booked," she explained.

"I hope you left a suite for our guest host?"

"There's one of the balcony suites booked for him and his crew."

"So everything is looking good from the sounds of it. Make sure our host has everything in his suite requested by his assistant. Remember, service is everything."

"We also have models coming in representing the CÎROC brand. So they'll mix in with our females as well. This will go well as long as everyone shows up."

"That's why I hired you, for your persistence to get the job done. You're always cracking the whip and making sure business is in line. If all this goes right, we'll make you a job change. Perhaps a new title and new position. Maybe GM over all the nightclubs."

"Incentive is always good," Melissa said, tapping on her iPad and then going over everything she needed to review.

Rosanna's phone sounded off and got her attention. When she looked down, the incoming call read Anonymous again. She needed to excuse herself to take the call. She had a feeling in her gut that it was the guy she had seen at the office.

"Excuse me, you two, I have to take this call," Rosanna said as she walked away to answer her phone.

Melissa continued to speak now that Rosanna's ears were not around.

"It's been awhile, you know, since we found each other's comfort. I would like some intimate incentive to get all of this done around here," she said, pointing to all the things she was taking care of in the club. "Plus, I know you miss this pretty kitty and my soft lips on your body," she said while licking her lips in a salacious manner to entice him.

"Yes, it has been some time."

"Four days is a long time when you're away from a good thing," she said, making him laugh as he took a look over his shoulder and saw that Rosanna was still tied up with her phone.

However, she didn't pay them any attention, because whoever was on the line with her had her a nervous wreck, which was another thing that stood out to him. She never took a call that necessitated her walking away from him, whether it be business or personal, which placed a thought into his mind that something was wrong. He didn't like when things were wrong or even felt wrong. It was just not good for finances or emotional and physical aspects of any relation or situation.

"Melissa, meet me in my office," he said.

His office was in the back of the fifty thousand-square-foot club.

The office boasted a black leather living room set that matched the chair behind his desk with gold TF initials stitched into the chair. Photographs of his lifetime of travels and celebrity associates covered the walls and allowed anyone who entered his office to live vicariously through him.

Melissa loved his power position and fit body, with which she enjoyed becoming intimate.

It didn't take long once he entered the office for her to come up to him and kiss his lips, before breaking from the kiss and taking his hand to guide him over to the couch. He didn't resist. He loved the sight of her butt in her red Dior jeans with black three-inch pumps by Vera Wang. The pumps even accentuated her curves. The white silk Dior top flowed over her breasts with now erect nipples, proof that her heart and body were aroused.

Once they made it over to the couch, she turned around to be greeted by more kisses. His hand pressed intimately onto her breasts, which created a welcoming pleasure that turned her on even more. His linen shirt slid off his body as her fingers assisted. They found their way to his pants, which she began to unbutton. She then moved back up and pulled off his tank top over his head and began to kiss his chest at the same time. She gracefully placed her soft lips on him and made his body come alive and at attention. Fully at a standstill, she stood and took off her clothing. She wanted him bad and knew they didn't have much time before Rosanna would be looking for him or one of the employees would be looking for her.

Seeing her flawless body in the nude, along with her perfect landing strip, he wanted all of her. With her eyes sparkling looking back at him, she caressed herself and licked her lips in a seductive way to lure him in even more. She lay on the couch and waved him over with her ass up facing him. She then turned to make eye contact with him as he entered strongly from behind and sent her a sensation.

"Mmmmh! Mmmh! Ahhhhh," she let out as her body started feeling good with him inside of her, going side to side, deeper and harder with each stroke.

Her mouth opened to allow the intimate breaths to spew out as she rocked back into him and felt all of his manhood please her body.

"Trae, Trae! Mmmmh! Mmmmh! Yessss, right there! Mmmmmh! Right there!" she moaned, like he needed guidance.

But he didn't need any direction. He knew her body better than she did. He knew how to please her with his fingers, tongue, and stick. She even came to his words over the phone while listening to his voice tell her what to do to her own body. She was into it then, just like she was now, loving and appreciating all of his stick.

Melissa had her three-guy rotation, and Travon was the only one to stay in the top three even after she got rid of the others.

Her body was really heating up now as she felt a surge of sensation race through her. She could feel the ultimate pleasure in her legs, stomach, heart, and kitty cat that was pulsating with sensation and surging through her like a wave of butterflies about to reach its peak of eruption.

"Oh God! Ooooh, ooooh! Aaaaah, aaaaah!. Mmmmmh! I, I, I'm cumming!" she yelled as she placed her head down and embraced the wave of orgasmic pleasure that surged through her and made every part of her body sensitive.

He continued pounding harder, deeper, and faster while squeezing her ass and feeling himself about to erupt in her tight wetness. He felt as if it was sucking on to him and feeling good to his body, the harder, deeper, and faster he stroked.

"Hmmmh! Hmmmh!" he let out when he felt the eruption escape him. His motion came to a slow halt as he squirted inside of her.

She squeezed him with her vagina and took all of him in, before looking over her shoulder at him.

"I hope you're done. We're going to get caught with all of this long stroking you're doing back there," she said.

"We're going to get caught with all of that moaning you're doing," he joked as he pulled out of her.

She turned all the way around to give him a little oral cleaning by taking him into her mouth. He didn't stop her, even as much as they wanted to stop so they would not get caught. She was good at what she was doing and he could not resist her touch, lips, or body. She finished kissing the head of it before grabbing her things and rushing off to the full bath with a shower behind the desk. He had it installed with the club for late nights, long days, and times just like this.

As he started to put on his clothes, there was a loud repetitious knock at the door. It was Rosanna. She placed her ear to the door and tried to listen in. Nothing. She even doubted that someone was inside after waiting for over ten minutes. The door finally swung open with Travon spraying Lysol air freshener in the air.

"Damn, mami, I can't take a shit in peace?" he said, trying to throw her off from suspecting anything. "What's so important that it has you banging on the door like this?" he said, still keeping her off guard, knowing she could be very jealous even if they weren't together.

Rosanna fanned the air because he was spraying in excess.

"You don't have to spray all of that shit like that! It's getting in my mouth," she said, trying to look past him. "Where's Melissa?" she asked, eyeing him up and down.

"Good question. Since I was using the bathroom, I figured she was going over some things with you about the bash we have this weekend, so you could relay all the details to me. Then again, you may have been too busy with the call you stepped away for," Travon said as he shifted the attention back to her, knowing the call in itself was something she dreaded. It was in her eyes and change of demeanor when he mentioned it. "You want to tell me something, Rosanna?" he asked, after seeing that she looked away when speaking to her.

"I do have something to tell you. I just don't want you to—"

"Rosanna!" Melissa called out.

Rosanna's head turned toward the voice yelling out for her. It was Melissa standing there with a smile on her face. She used another door in the office to exit, only to come around to the front. It was a perfect strategy, especially after hearing Rosanna ask about her whereabouts.

"We can go over the finer details of what each VIP requests for their suites, or you can check in tomorrow so you can relay the details to Travon."

Rosanna was shocked and caught off guard when she saw Melissa come from behind her, since she didn't remember seeing her after she got off the phone. She took out her iPhone and scrolled through it to her Appointments section.

"Okay, I'll schedule a meeting with you around

1:00 p.m."

"One is good for me," she responded.

"Ladies, is there anything else you two need to talk about for now, because we have to go," Travon said while looking at his watch.

He always wanted to be on time and stay on schedule. Rosanna followed behind him as they started to make their way out of the club. He briefly cut his eyes over to Melissa as his thoughts flashed back to their intimate encounter they just had in the office.

On the other hand, Rosanna was thinking about how she wanted to express her dark secret to him before she was interrupted. *Maybe that was a sign not to say anything*, she thought as they exited the club. But he had to know before it was too late. Another thought entered her mind that also tormented her. She knew that she needed to make a decision.

## Chapter 7

At 5:47 p.m., Sarah was at home staring in the mirror eyeing herself up and down. She wanted to make sure she was looking the part for her dinner date with Travon. Although she was a country girl, she knew how to be a lady and dress the part. Tonight she put on red denim jeans with gold stitching by Dior Homme that flowed over her country curves down to her three-inch Red Bottoms and a silk white blouse by Versace with a floral print around the breast area. Her hair was pulled back and displayed her facial features and sparkling eyes that were perfectly accented by her white, gold, and black eye shadow and black eye liner. Her beauty was multiplied and gave her a completely different look than when Travon had first seen her that morning.

She glanced down at her Movado watch that flowed with her overall look. The bezel had eight carats of diamonds around that matched her two-carat stud earrings. Before leaving the bathroom, she blew a kiss to herself in the mirror before heading downstairs to go have dinner with Travon—the man that one day would be all hers. Or at least that's what she was thinking before her cell phone rang. She looked down at the screen.

"Oh, your timing is so bad," she said when she saw that it was someone from her past, a friend, so to speak. "Hello, darling," she said when answering the phone.

"It's me, Tom Carter."

"I know who you are, fool. Remember these phones have caller ID. Now, what are you calling me for?"

"I was thinking about coming to see how you're settling in."

*No, not now!* she thought. She hadn't even had a chance to know Travon. "I don't think your presence is a good idea at this point."

"That's what all you women say when you get distracted. So I take it you have met someone?"

"You can say that. So don't come ruining anything just yet. Let me get situated, and I promise to invite you up. Maybe even to meet my new friend," she said, before a silence fell briefly as she waited for his response.

"I'll give you some time. Just don't lose yourself in the new environment. People tend to do that," he responded, before hanging up and leaving her to think about his last words.

However, only Travon was on her mind.

Tom was a good friend of hers, and he didn't like that she chose to relocate or that he would not see her as much. But she felt the move was for the better.

"Dumb ass," she said, not liking that he hung up on her abruptly.

She didn't let it bother her too much because thoughts of how her night with Travon might go kept entering her mind.

A horn sounded off in front of the house. She made her way to the door and opened it, only to see a charcoal-gray Rolls Royce Ghost with tinted windows concealing the driver. Right then, the window started to slowly roll down to reveal Rosanna's face. Sarah's face went from happy to curious when she saw the same Latina from that morning.

She blew the horn again and stared back at Sarah before swaying her head to gesture for her to come on out. She looked around her house and made sure everything was in order before stepping out, securing the door, and then making her way over to the car.

Rosanna gave her a female's head-to-toe once-over and checked out her sense of style and fashion.

"Why are you blaring the horn like that? And do you not think you're parked in front of the wrong house?" she said when she saw the fancy car parked in front of her house instead of Travon's house.

"I'm here to pick you up and take you to dinner with Travon. So get in, because he is not too fond of being stood up or people being late," Rosanna warned.

She really didn't want to be the one picking up Sarah and taking her to the man she had feelings for, but this was her job, and what she was feeling was personal.

On the other hand, Sarah was confused when she looked over at Travon's house. She thought: *He said he was going to cook dinner himself, so what changed?*

Rosanna saw the confusion on her face and felt a need to inform her.

"Never try to predict him or figure out what he likes and dislikes. He'll let you know about that when you two have dinner. Now get in," Rosanna said.

Sarah made her way around to the passenger side and prepared to get into the back of the car until Rosanna stopped her.

"Hell no! I'm not your chauffeur, mami! I'm taking you for a ride, and that's it. I'm only doing this for my boss."

"Forgive me, sweetheart. This fancy car thing is new to me," Sarah said genuinely dumbfounded by her actions at that moment.

She got into the front seat and felt somewhat nervous and curious at the same time. She remembered that Connie said Travon was a mystery.

Rosanna pulled off and headed to Travon's other place.

"What's your name?" Sarah asked, trying to have a casual conversation.

"I know who you are and what you're doing trying to get close to him. I won't let it happen," Rosanna said smoothly before briefly cutting her eye over at Sarah.

Sarah instantly felt the tension between the two of them now. At the same time, she wondered exactly where she was going with this lady that seemed to have an attitude.

"I have no secrets or negligent intentions. So you can assume you know me when you don't. Now that you opened your mouth, I know who you are, or should I say, I think you are, since people tend to change," Sarah said, fighting back with her words of sarcasm.

She flipped the sun visor down and looked into the mirror. She puckered her lips and winked at herself. She loved her comeback toward Rosanna.

"I will be keeping a close watch on you. Mr. Robinson will be informed since it's my job to protect his best interest and assets," Rosanna said.

Sarah gave off a light laugh that angered Rosanna even more as she started cussing in

Spanish before turning the Latin music on.

Rosanna was taking Sarah to the mansion, which was a place Rosanna deemed as her place to go when he once shared her time and space. His home in the Pinehurst Estates boasted ten thousand square feet of opulence with three fireplaces, six full bathrooms, three half baths, a game room, a home theater, a gym, and more. It all catered to his need of entertaining guests on another level. It was a home that he kept as his getaway for times like tonight. Rosanna didn't want anyone to ever come between her and Travon, but their unique bond was just that, and it would be no more.

Sarah also didn't want anyone to stand in the way of her getting to know Travon better, or her time with him so she could make a mental, physical, and emotional connection with him. In her eyes, and knowing what she knew, he was unique and captivating.

## Chapter 8

The car ride to Travon's mansion was filled with tension and thoughts of each woman being with the one man they both wanted all to themselves.

When Rosanna pulled up to the mansion, she could not wait until Sarah exited the car so she could go on with her night.

"You can get out now!" Rosanna said aggressively and with arrogance while not even looking at her.

"Well, sweetheart, you need to think about getting a different job or a man in your life to release some of that tension you have building up," Sarah said, sending her words with a vacuous smile of sarcasm that taunted Rosanna.

It made Rosanna angry, and she pulled off fast, leaving Sarah and Travon to enjoy their dinner date.

Travon stood at the door checking the time on his black pearl-faced Movado watch with a white gold case and band. The watch flowed with his overall look of a white silk short-sleeve button-up shirt with white gold buttons outlined in 18-karat gold with a Versace print on the left side. His light denim YSL pants added to his look with a pair of suede Armani loafers.

Sarah saw him light up with a smile, and she felt warm inside and welcomed by his presence when he greeted her at the door.

"I hope you brought your appetite tonight," he said.

"I could eat a horse with a side of potatoes," Sarah said with her Southern drawl.

"You're in luck, we have horse on the menu tonight," he said jokingly, which made her laugh and at the same time tap him lightly on the arm.

"Is this your house, too?"

"One of many."

"You only need one with everything you need, just like having only one woman that gets and understands you. The one that gives you all the comfort you desire, and the place where your heart and mind call home," she said, sending her poetic charm his way with a smile backed by the sparkle in her eyes.

Without question, he enjoyed her words and the look in her eyes. She was different, truly unlike those before her as this feeling of something new came over him.

"Can I take your hand and lead you to the dining room?"

"Please do, darling," she responded, extending her hand for him to lead her into the dining room as well as into his heart and mind.

Her soft hand embraced his masculine hand as they made their way through the mansion. She took in all of the view of the art, marble floors, and imported statues along with other custom unique features of a wealthy businessman.

"Whatever is cooking sure smells good. I hope it tastes as good as it smells, meaning you better be a good cook and know your way around the kitchen," she said, being bold and funny all in the same sense.

"I assure you'll love the presentation of what we're eating tonight. As for me knowing my way around the kitchen, I know my way around in there; however, tonight I have my chef, Crystal, and her staff displaying their five-star skills."

As those words flowed from his mouth, they entered the dining room where she became impressed by the layout and elegance of the table setting.

"This is truly thoughtful and beautiful. Better looking than any restaurant I've ever been in," she said, taking it all in and appreciating the lit red candles centering the table of glass with a custom marble base.

The silverware was trimmed in 24-karat gold as were the wine glasses and fine imported China dishes off to the side in the cabinet. He pulled her chair out and allowed her to take a seat.

"You're really a gentleman. I like this in you," she said, almost giggling at the thought of the romantic evening.

"I'm always at my best when there's a lady around," he responded, which got a smile from her.

Chef Crystal came out to address the meal order for the dinner tonight. Crystal was thirty-two years old and had blonde hair, blue eyes, and a golden tan from lying out when she was not in the kitchen perfecting her craft. The five-foot-eight beauty was precocious in the chef world. She was always creative and tried new things to impress her clients as well as the culinary world when she was blogging and posting pictures on her social media site.

"Mr. Robinson, are you ready for your appetizers?" she questioned.

"Yes, please. My guest tells me she is ready to eat a horse," he responded.

Sarah felt slightly embarrassed yet found it funny, but she still wanted to cover his mouth for repeating her words.

The server came out with a bottle of Chateau du Busca Hors d'Age. His staff poured drinks for the two of them.

"This should compliment your appetizers, sir."

As if his words were the cue, the other server came out with the appetizers.

"Here we have fresh portabella mushrooms

stuffed with fresh blue crab brought in from Maryland today. The sauce is a creamy garlic puree with tomatoes, onions, red chili, and jalapeño peppers to give it a little spice and excitement to start this evening's meal."

"Thank you, Chris," Travon said, waiting for Sarah to try the food.

She took a bite and allowed it to wake up her taste buds.

"Mmmmh! This is so good. Excuse me for speaking with food in my mouth," she said before taking another bite of the deliciously prepared stuffed mushroom.

She closed her eyes and enjoyed the taste that left a euphoric sensation in her mouth as a smile formed. She then opened her eyes to take a sip of her wine that seemed to flow smoothly over her tongue, chasing down the blue crab that complemented the flavor just as the server had said.

She made eye contact with Travon, who was enjoying himself as well.

"I could get used to this good cooking. I don't know, but I may have to marry your chef if she is into it," Sarah said jokingly.

He truly appreciated her presence because she didn't feel like she was forcing herself or anything on him. He covered his mouth laughing at how silly she was.

"Very funny. I was starting to think it was me you really wanted."

Her eyes found his and took in his words. They shared a brief moment of smiles as their eyes seemed to speak without having said a word.

"How's the food, Mr. Robinson?" Crystal asked as she came out from the kitchen to check on her client.

"It's the best in the world, which is why I enjoy having you as my chef. Now my guest is thinking about marrying you to have a lifetime supply of your great cooking."

Both women became slightly embarrassed and smiled it off. At the same time, the chef appreciated the compliment before heading back to the kitchen to continue her work.

"You are loose lips telling her I want to marry her."

"It's funny; besides, you can have me and she'll cook for you every night anyway."

Her eyes lit up as she took another bite of her appetizer.

"I'm okay with that. Now tell me why you're single, because I already know why I'm single. Also, why does one man need a big place like this with no one to share his happiness with?"

"I'm single by choice, because I've been

through a lot. I opened up and trusted the wrong people, but now I feel like I can invite someone into my space that can handle all that I am and what I bring," he explained while looking into her eyes and making full contact.

"That's similar to what has happened to me. The only thing I have to add to that is my father passed away; and with me being the only child, it took a toll on me. So I moved up North to start all over to see what life brings."

"Well, fate has brought you and me together today, and I'm thankful for having you share this dinner tonight in this big house as you stated. Therefore, we don't have to be alone in this house or this world," he said, allowing his genuine words to flow into her ear and down to her heart. He took a sip of his wine before saying more, since he wanted to connect with her by expressing to her who he was. "I don't allow too many people to get close to me for many reasons. I love the concept of love, you know the institution of a relationship; but it's the pain that comes with it when things don't work out that I find myself avoiding. But now I'm ready to embrace it and all that comes with the world's most intricate emotion," he said, finding the right words to caress her heart and mind.

She was now open to him and ready to express herself just as he had done, but in more ways. This is the man she had been looking for, for many years. Unfortunately, it was the same man that Rosanna was looking for until she got twisted up in the wrong direction.

"Can I hold your hand?" she asked him, wanting to be closer and intimate.

He obliged even though he was surprised that she had asked him. Holding his hand placed her back in a place of comfort. Her eyes then locked in on his, and they both could feel the connection.

"You're a good man and good things will come to you. I'm not talking about all of this—the house and cars—but good, meaning the right woman who listens and knows what you need and desire. We've experienced some of the same problems in life, but together we can share some of the greater days that remain. We can come alive as one if we allow that wall to come down to see the world of emotional promise that awaits us," she said, feeling like her hand was melting inside of his.

He felt the affection in her words as her eyes sparkled with passion, with a little lust for love. Most women didn't approach him like this because they saw the flashy cars and house and thought they were dealing with a sugar daddy or something, which made him fuck 'em and leave 'em for the most part.

However, Sarah's mind-set was different.

There was something about her that seemed just right. *Or could she be too good to be true?* he thought. But at the same time, he didn't want to keep her at bay too long just in case she was the one good girl willing to be for him and about him and their relationship.

"Sarah, a relationship and love are an investment of time and emotion. You get out of it what you put into it. Both parties have to be on the same page at all times. No lies, no games, and no secrets. If either party does not abide by the three things I just mentioned, then they're at a loss of time and emotion. And that's how people get hurt," he said, wanting to pull her closer to kiss or be intimate.

She could feel the butterflies in her stomach and heart as each word came out of his mouth. This was truly the beginning of a great evening of food, conversation, and smiles. It was a true portrait of romance.

## Chapter 9

After dinner they made their way into the formal living room where more candles were lit, Korbel Gold champagne sat on ice, and chocolate-covered strawberries were accompanied by Hershey's Kisses.

"I never had chocolate-covered strawberries before. I mean, I've read about them in a magazine with romance stories."

"I bet the magazine and stories didn't tell you that you only share this desert with someone you view as special," he said while pouring a glass of champagne for the two of them.

"They didn't mention anything about a good-looking man trying to get me drunk with alcohol and his smooth words," she joked, with a smile which proved that she appreciated him and his every word.

"Really? That's how you feel?"

"I'm not complaining. I'm simply enjoying the entertainment, especially the view of you sitting beside me."

"Well, let's make a toast to a good night and me continuing to entertain you as you said."

She was smiling ear to ear and taking it all in as their glasses chimed together for the toast. They both had a sip, and then Travon grabbed a strawberry covered in milk chocolate.

"Can I treat you to dessert?" he asked while

holding onto the strawberry.

"Yes, please," she responded in a soft warm and welcoming tone. He place the passion fruit up to her puckered lips. She opened her mouth, took a bite, and then allowed the flavors to erupt in her mouth, stimulating her thoughts and feelings of the moment. "Mmmh!"

"Now chase it with the champagne," he said, guiding her down the road to passion. She obliged only to discover another euphoric food moment, or food foreplay, so to speak.

"You're a true gentleman right now, but how long does this treatment last in a relationship?"

"It depends on how long the lucky lady sticks around. Like I said, it's never me; it's the people I trust," he responded while eating the other half of the strawberry.

He chased it down with his champagne before placing his glass alongside Sarah's finished glass. He refilled both glasses. She drank half of hers before taking another strawberry covered in chocolate.

"Now it's my turn, Travon. Close your eyes," she said, giving him a salacious look before she puckered her lips. He did as she requested. "Share this taste of pleasure with me," she said.

She leaned in close and placed one end of the sweet chocolate-covered strawberry in her mouth and then moved forward until the fruit touched his lips. He could feel the warmth of her face closing in on his, which made the moment even more intimate. He bit into the fruit and allowed her lips to touch his. Food foreplay. The wine and champagne flowed through their bodies, which gave each of them a nice warm buzz that made the kiss even more explosive as their lips interlocked and ignited a rush in their bodies. It took their hearts and minds to a comforting yet sensual place. Her hands then found his neck to caress as his hands pulled her body closer.

"Mmmmmh! Mmmh!" she let out a vibrating sensation over his tongue, loving his kiss and touch.

*It feels so good, but this is so wrong. It's not supposed to be this way. But he was that good. Is this how all women feel about him when they're in his presence? I don't care. I never felt this way about anyone or this way before. Wrong or not, I don't want this to stop, at least not now*, she thought to herself as her hands slid down his biceps and then over his chest. It was her playground—her treasure. It had been over two years since she'd been with a man physically or emotionally. She didn't even have the time to pleasure herself, or simply just was not in the mood or that type.

But right now in this very heated moment, her sexual alarm was going off as hormones heated up with each passing of his hands over her soft, sensitive body. She yearned for Travon to be her fireman and put out this sexual fire. His hands found her breasts, and she moaned aloud when he cupped them.

"Mmmmmh!"

She pushed him back onto the couch to take control as the burning desire to be pleased was overwhelming her inside and out. She could feel his rock-hard love stick press against his pants onto her love spot. She wanted him. She didn't want this to stop here as a feeling was rising in her body. The butterflies of her heart beat fast, and the pulsating sensation in her body turned her on and made her wet. She wanted all of him now.

The doorbell rang back to back. She heard it but didn't want to stop because it was not her problem. She was too focused on him right now. He heard it. He prepared to bring a pause to this moment of passion until she undid his pants and slid her hand under his silk boxers. She struck sexual gold when she grabbed his hard, long pole of passion. When she felt how thick and long he was, it made her heart thump with excitement and even more sexual desire to have all of him. She reached down further and could not believe it. *He is easily eleven or twelve inches. That's not normal. Then again, he's not normal in any other way*, she thought.

Her love spot became so wet with his manhood in her hand, especially never having been with a man so well endowed. Of course, it also had been awhile since her pleasure spot had seen any action. The doorbell sounded off again. He didn't want to answer it with her soft hand on his manhood. She pulled it out of his pants and took a visual look at this sexual treasure. She pulled away from the intense passionate kissing as both of them now looked at one another and felt different. It was a very special feeling. The look in her eyes was full of lust and passion.

"You can answer that if you want," she said while massaging his love stick and contemplating if she wanted that thing inside of her right now. Almost teasing him, she said, "I'll still be here waiting on you when you come back."

There was a smile on her lips, eyes, and heart. There was a true connection between the two of them.

The doorbell sounded off again. This time, he sat up and she removed her hand. He got up and walked away awkwardly while he tried to adjust himself from being so stiff.

As he made his way to the door, he thought

that it probably was Rosanna, until he came closer to the door and he could see out. But there was no one there. He opened the door and looked at the mansions to the right and left of his, but nothing. There was no one in sight. They must have gotten tired of waiting, that or the bad-ass kids in the neighborhood had played with the doorbell and then ran, which was a game he played as a child. He shut the door to make his way back to Sarah, who was ready to continue what she had started.

As he entered the room, she was finishing up a phone call. She then set down her cell phone beside the strawberries. Her back was to him, so she didn't see him walk back inside. For some strange reason, he stopped in his tracks as if he wanted to catch her doing something negligent. Maybe he wanted to know who she was talking to. *Did the caller have something to do with the doorbell ringing? Or am I just paranoid?* he questioned himself, since he was always on high alert. As he stood there, she began to undress and let her clothes fall gracefully to the floor. She slid out of her pants, bra, and panties, and then she took her champagne and drank the rest of it.

"Perfection at its best," he said as he walked over to her bare body standing freshly undressed.

She turned toward his voice and looked over her shoulder and smiled. He approached her and took off his pants to be in the same space as she was. Together, they were a picture of intimate art. He came around to the front of her. She reached her hand up to his chest and appreciated his toned frame.

"It's your playground, so have fun with it," he joked.

She leaned in closer and placed kisses onto his chest as her soft hands found his love stick once more and massaged it to its full potential. With his long thickness in her hand, she brought it close and rubbed her pretty kitty that was pulsating and wanting him. Her heart thumped at the feeling of his thick long love stick rubbing against her clitoris, which turned her on even more. Her eyes closed and embraced the sensation that seemed so wrong, yet felt so good. His hands roamed her body while his lips found her neck. There was heavy, intense petting until he lifted her up with ease. Her right arm wrapped around his neck and she held on. Her left arm was free, and she reached down and guided his firm love stick into her tightness. Her heart and body could feel a wave of butterflies stream through her as his love stick entered her and filled up all of her body, making her wet and tight love fit like a glove.

"Aaaaaah!" she let out, before burying her face into his neck and squeezing him tightly.

She could feel the pressure of his long, thick treasure inside of her as he raised her body up and down on his manhood. She squeezed her ass and loved the feeling just as much as she embraced it.

She could feel her body stretching to accommodate his love stick; at the same time, her body appreciated the feeling it was giving her as the fluttering sensation streamed through her body.

"Aaaaaah, aaaahh, aaaaaah, mmmh, mmmmh!" she let out in between passionate kisses and love bites to his neck.

She was overwhelmed by the pleasure she was experiencing. Now with both hands around his neck, the ride picked up just as the sensation did. He could feel himself hitting her insides no matter what angle it was, and he loved it because she was so appreciative.

"I like the way your body feels," he said to her while still gripping her ass and lifting her up and down on his long, thick love stick.

"Yesssss! Mmmmh! Yesss! Me too," she let out in agreement with him.

He understood. Her body felt better than Melissa's, Rosanna's, or any other girl's he had been with. This feeling alone made this sex good. He could never tell her that her pussy was that good. He would just enjoy it every time.

"Ohhhh, ohhhh! Oh my God! Mmmmh! Mmmh!" she screamed as a continuous surging sensation raced through her body and made her feel the orgasmic feeling that was rushing through her body and ready to escape.

She'd never felt this way before. It was his size, good looks, wealth, the motion sticking it to her side to side, deeper and harder, and the fact that he was the first black guy she had ever been with. The curiosity had not killed that cat but lured her pretty kitty in as she would say. With him being black, it made her want him even more. Since she was from down South, it was like a forbidden fruit she desired but could never have until now.

"Trae! Mmmmmh! Mmmmmh! This feels so good! Mmmh! Mmmh!"

It was music to his ears that made him pick up his movement. He turned around and found the couch where he laid her down to have more leverage. He placed her left leg over his right shoulder and stroked her deep, hitting the back walls and her spot in repetition.

"Aaah, aaah, aaah, aaah, aaah, aaah, aaah!"

Her moans continued to sound like music to his ears, which allowed him to know that he was doing the right motions to please her in every way. His heart was beating fast while he looked on at her natural beauty and the lust and intimacy in her as he stroked faster, harder, and deeper. He connected with her as they continued looking into one another's eyes, which made this intimate moment more pleasurable. At the same time, they both felt an enhancing sensation that was coming from within their hearts as their minds visually captured the promise of a good thing in each other. Could this be love at first sight or simply the best sex ever?

"Put my leg down so you can come close to me," she said, wanting to be more intimate and close.

She wrapped her legs around him and felt the intense wave of orgasm surge through her body ready to be released. It was coming. She could feel it in her heart, her legs, her stomach, and her wet kitty. She could not hold it back any more.

"Ohhh, Trae! Mmmmmh! Mmmmmh! Mmmmmmh! Aaaaaaah, I'm cumming! Mmmmmh!" she moaned.

She was unable to hold it back any more, yet she loved the back-to-back wave of multiple orgasms that had taken over her body and made her heart flutter with passion. Her stomach filled with the sensation of butterflies as her body released over and over, making her pretty kitty wetter and wetter.

Her intense moans and the feeling of her body squirting from cumming made him continue to stroke harder, deeper, and faster. He felt himself about to cum as well. His breathing picked up, his grip on her body tightened, and his thick love stick was at its max, pulsating thickness and length with each stroke that was bringing him closer to blasting off.

"Here I come, baby," he said while slamming into her love spot with passion over and over while busting inside of her.

He was still stroking fast, deep, and hard before slowing down and then coming to a slow stroke that still made her moan lightly. She then stopped moaning, only to breathe heavily and heatedly as multiple orgasms continued racing through her body at a pulsating rate. He gave her the greatest pleasure and sensation in the world as if multiple fingers and tongues were all over her body and wetness. As the striking waves of multiple orgasms continued erupting from her body, she held on to him tightly. She never wanted him to leave, and she never wanted this moment to end.

"Don't move, Trae. Just hold me, please," she finally let out, still sensitive and still cumming.

He wanted to get up just to see her face to see if she was really serious or crazy. A few minutes passed before the ultimate pleasure came to an end, which allowed her to speak with ease and show a smile on her heart, face, and body.

"Thank you, Trae," she said before kissing his ear and then his neck.

Her Southern belle accent made him appreciate her even more.

"Are you thanking me for dinner or dessert?" he joked.

She laughed and placed more kisses on his neck, ear, and then his lips.

"Thank you for treating me and my body like a woman," she said while kissing his lips again. "I could really get used to having this all the time. I just hope you don't think I was too easy, or like the rest of the women you encounter. By the way, it has been two years since I was with anyone. Just so you know what type of woman I am."

"You have my attention at this very moment, and not just physically," he told her.

*Wow!* she thought as her heart smiled upon hearing this. She kissed him again.

"Normally I would ask you to leave, but I'm inviting you to the shower and to stay the night if you would like," he said while kissing her lips and neck, and then down to her breasts and then her stomach before stopping.

He could see she loved the idea of where his

lips and tongue were about to go until he stopped teasing her.

"We can finish in the shower if you like. You would be the first female to stay the night," he said as he got up from her and allowed his manhood to swing as he walked toward the master bedroom.

"Thank you again, because I knew there was something special about you that I couldn't just pass up," she said, getting up and taking her cell phone.

She typed in a quick message and sent it to the person she was talking with before Travon had come back into the room. She placed the phone back on the table, only to hurry behind him before he turned back around. The night for them was still young and full of more sexual pleasure and passion—from the shower to the bed room, then followed by pillow talk. This allowed them to connect on a more mental and emotional level that seemed to be different from those they had chosen before them.

## Chapter 10

The morning hour came quick. Rosanna would normally be the one to pick him up for business; instead, his other assistant, Jennifer, showed up in his all-white Range Rover Sport with tinted windows, TV in the dash, and two thirteen-inch flats that flipped down in the back for the passengers to view or when Travon used the screen with his laptop.

Travon was just getting out of the shower when the house phone rang. He knew he was pressed for time since he got up a little late, so he exited the bathroom and made his way over to the phone.

"Mmmh! You look sexy!" Sarah said, lying in bed barely covered with the white satin sheets that felt cool to her flesh.

Travon simply smiled at her before answering the phone.

"Hello."

"Mr. Robinson, good morning, sir. This is Jennifer. I'm out front waiting on you to start your day."

His face frowned briefly and wondered why Rosanna was not picking him up.

"Where's Rosanna?"

"She said she needed to take care of something but would be back around later."

"All right, I'll be down. I just got out of the

shower, so give me some time, please?"

"No problem, sir," she responded with a smile before hanging up and having thoughts of him getting out of the shower enter her mind.

She secretly admired her boss, but never thought about pursuing him because of her fear of getting rejected or fired.

Travon was back inside the mansion getting dressed while Sarah gathered her things.

"I'll shower once I get home," Sarah said, even though she didn't want to leave.

She really wanted to cook him breakfast and then have dinner waiting when he came home after a long day of work. She also wanted to show him how much she appreciated him as well as that she desired him more than for just sex.

"I know you said I was the first to stay the night, but will I have another chance to do it all over again, so I can be the only woman to stay two nights?" she asked with a smile.

"Let's see how it plays out. Oh, your phone is right there. It was going off when I woke up. I didn't wake you for it, since I figured they would call you back if it was important."

For some strange reason, her heart started picking up its pace as her mind raced while thinking the worse. She knew who was calling her. She just hoped Travon didn't check the voicemail, caller ID, or text messages. If he did, it was not displayed on his face or in his current actions. She managed to smile through her concern.

"Thank you," she said as she walked over to grab her phone.

Travon was one for observation and a good judge of people's characters, which was how he surveyed people in the business world. He picked up on her shift in demeanor, which made his guard go up a little to give him a chance to figure out what was going on, if anything at all.

"Come here, beautiful," he said as he turned around and placed his lips on hers and then her forehead. "I do like you, for the record, and what I see in you is potentially more than I have witnessed in anyone else, especially since I just kissed you with morning breath," he joked.

She laughed and slapped him lightly on his chest.

"I look forward to mornings under the covers with you, followed by good morning wake-up sex with a little breakfast in bed," Sarah said while rubbing his chest and looking into his eyes.

She could feel a unique connection with him. It was a tortuous situation she found herself in with him.

"Let's get out of here before we get stuck in this bedroom doing things we'll definitely enjoy.

Then I'll regret missing out on my meeting and conducting business," he said before kissing her lips again. "Last kiss until we meet again. When I'm outside of the house and workplace, I keep it business because I'm really private. I hope you can respect where I stand?"

"You're not a PDA-type guy," she said, meaning public display of affection.

He was but just not right away in case things didn't work out. Then he would feel embarrassed for giving a woman the world, who didn't appreciate him and all that he brought. He felt that it was all about timing and knowing when to say and do things.

Travon also felt that if they respected this one wish, they would desire him more in the long run, since they could not be able to have him anywhere and everywhere. Also, for the one woman or women he decided to see, he didn't want everyone to know how good he was because then they would desire him as well. So they respected him, which added to the chase of him and all that he brought.

"I do respect you and your decision. Now give me another kiss so I can savor it until the next time," she said with her Southern accent that charmed him. So he made the kiss even more passionate, and they felt the rush of emotions during the intimate moment. “I cannot wait to have more of you and your time.”

“We have to stop kissing like that before we end up back in the bedroom,” he said while holding her soft body in his embrace.

“You’re right. We don’t want to start something we can’t finish,” she said, allowing her hand to caress his manhood as she spoke to it. “I’ll be good until you come back around.”

He laughed and found it sexy and funny at the same time. He never had a woman talk to his love stick.

“You’re a bad little country girl, huh?” he said.

“A good bad, not a bad bad,” she said.

“Let’s go before you turn me into your love slave and I never get any work done.”

*I got him! He is all mine now*, she thought. *Can I really have him and this life he lives? Will Tom Carter allow this to take place? What would he think?* He wanted to keep a leash on her, because he felt he knew best.

## Chapter 11

Rosanna was at her place in Hershey Heights in Hershey, Pennsylvania, located just minutes from Harrisburg. She was mentally and emotionally wrecked and torn between two worlds: one man and two aspects—business and personal. Rosanna was a mother of a four-year-old baby boy, Jamir Robinson, who was nicknamed JR. His father was Travon. However, they kept this a secret. Only he and Rosanna were aware of him being his son. Even Rosanna's own family didn't know who the child's father was, other than that he was American and did right by him and gave him anything and everything he desired, especially his time. Travon knew that being a father figure was vital to a child's growth and life experiences.

Rosanna's son was a true gift to her; however, having him did compromise her life and future, especially since she was unable to live as she wanted or love the man with whom she had the child. This intricate and unwieldy situation was eating at her emotionally and mentally as she tried to figure Travon out and it out all at the same time. She had been patient for so long and invested time and emotions into Travon, but she also placed her trust in him as she followed her instincts.

Rosanna felt that with all the time she gave

Travon, and even a son, he would want her more than he desired any other woman; but somehow or somewhere in the last five years, their relationship fell apart, even though the intimacy was there when they made love. He was a good man to her and a good father, but working closely together every day, and all day, maybe forced them apart in the long run somehow. Yet they still had a unique bond because of their son and a never-dying love and respect for one another.

Sitting on the edge of her son's bed as he was watching cartoons, Rosanna started to realize that if she walked away from Travon, she would still have a reflection of him in their son every time she looked into his eyes.

Jamir was so young and innocent. When he turned around from his cartoon watching, he saw his mother looked distraught.

"Are you okay, mama?"

"It's nothing, Son. Mama loves you."

"I know, mama, you tell me every day."

"I will love you forever, son."

"How long do I have to stay with Abuela?"

"Not long; besides, you can have fun with Abuela."

"Papi told me he was taking me to Disney World. I don't want to miss Mickey Mouse."

"When did he say that?"

"Yesterday."

Rosanna was really torn, since she was unaware of this trip that Travon had planned with their son. *Why didn't he tell me?* she wondered. *Is our relationship falling that far apart*? she questioned, not knowing why their overall relationship had gotten to this point.

"Abuela should be here any minute, so make sure you have the toys and things you want to play with ready to go, okay?"

"Yes, mami."

Rosanna embraced his innocence as he continued to watch cartoons. She then flashed back down memory lane and looked at the picture of Travon and Jamir at the playground spending time together and having fun. *What happened to those happy times?* she wondered.

If Travon knew what she was planning on doing, good times would be far from her mind.

All of her thoughts came to a halt when her cell phone started ringing, followed by a knock at her front door. Her nerves started to get the best of her as her heart and mind began to race while trying to figure out what she needed to do in the best interest of her son and herself.

"Who's that, mama?" he asked, after hearing the knock on the door as well as her cell phone go off.

"I don't know. Hang on a minute," she said as she made her way into the living room to get her cell phone.

It was a call she was not ready to take just yet. She needed to get her thoughts all in order. She wanted to make the right decision that would benefit her and her son, especially knowing his relationship with his father. She sent the call to voicemail because she didn't want to deal with it just yet.

She answered the door and saw her mother standing there with a partial smile, because she could feel that there was something wrong with her daughter. She could also hear it in her voice, and now see the look in her eyes and with her body language.

"Rosanna, I'm worried about you," her mother said, opening her arms to embrace her daughter with motherly love. "Give me a hug."

Rosanna did just what her mother said. She wanted to feel her mother's comfort and love.

"Don't worry, Mama, I'll be just fine."

"That's what your mouth says, but it's not true. You've never been a good liar even as a kid!" her mother said, making her give off light laughter through her tormented thoughts and emotions.

At the same time, she thought back to when she told her mother, Maria, that she was not with a certain guy as a teenage girl, but her mother knew from all the tell-tale signs.

Little did Rosanna's mother know, but she had been living a lie for over five years.

"Where's my grandson?"

"He was back there in the room watching cartoons. JR, Abuela is here!" Rosanna called out to him.

He came running up fast behind her. He was happy and full of innocence.

"Abuela!" he said while jumping up into her arms.

She kissed him on his cheeks and hugged him with a grandmother's love.

"Oh my, you're getting bigger every time I see you."

"I'm getting stronger, too, Abuela. I lift the suitcase that Mama put my clothes in," he said full of excitement.

Maria held him with love.

"My boy, we're going to make your favorite chocolate chip cookies."

"I like those, Abuela."

"I know," she said while kissing him on the forehead. "Rosanna, call me this afternoon. I want to know what you have going on and how you're really feeling. Okay?"

"Yes, Mama. Here is JR's clothing and some

money for him."

Maria heard that money was coming with her too, which made her really worry.

"Don't say it, ma. I see the look on your face," Rosanna said, not wanting to go into details while her son was present. She also needed to get out of the house for now or go back to work. "I promise I'll call you later," she said, kissing her mother on the cheek and then her son.

"Grandson, you ready to make some cookies?"

"Yes, chocolate chip."

"I'll see both of you later on, okay, ma?"

"Mama, tell Papi I'm with Abuela so he can pick me up for Disney World," JR said, all excited about the trip.

"I'll tell him you love him so much and cannot wait to see him. Now go with Abuela. I love you, baby."

"I love you more, Mama," he said with all his little heart and innocence.

Once they left the condo, Rosanna stood still and looked around. She felt a void in her life and heart. At the same time, emotions streamed through her body, tormenting her.

Her cell phone sounded off, which brought all of her thoughts and focus back to the phone and the caller ID. As her paranoia kicked in, she raced over to the window and peeped out. There was nothing. No one. When the phone stopped ringing, it only added more paranoia as thoughts rapidly entered her mind. Suddenly a knock came across the front door, followed by the doorbell. Now her heart and mind raced as she tried to figure out what she needed to do if the person on the other side of the door was who she thought it was. At the same time, she hoped it was not Travon coming to check up on her, because he would be pissed that his son was not present, and she didn't want to fight with him about him not being here.

She made her way to the door and looked through the peephole and saw a face all too familiar. She took a deep breath and opened the door. At the same time, she forced a vacuous smile of deception. The male standing on the other side of the door looked serious, clean-cut, and formal.

"I think we need to talk," he said as he walked past her into the living room.

She closed her eyes and the door at the same time, dreading this very moment which she had tried to avoid for many years.

## Chapter 12

Over at Global Image Group, Travon was in his office going over today's events with Jennifer. A part of his mind was still on last night's fireworks with Sarah, while the other part was on his long-time assistant, friend, and mother of his child, Rosanna. He wondered why she had unexpectedly opted out of work today like she did, but there was business as usual that he needed to take care of.

"Not to cut you off from what you're doing, Jennifer, but you didn't say why Rosanna didn't show up today, and I don't have it over here with the rest of my messages," Travon said.

"She didn't give any details other than she would be around later."

"Okay," he said while looking on at his vintage BR120 Sport Bell & Ross Aviation watch. It was a nice timepiece. "Excuse me for a minute, Jennifer, I need you to step out briefly, please," he asked after having a thought of paranoia and concern, especially since he was not one for out-of-line behavior.

As she stepped out, he picked up the phone and speed-dialed Rosanna. It rang a few times, only to go to voicemail. He called again just to be sure—the same thing. His mind was now thinking the worst. He wanted to know where she was and why she was not answering her phone.

In the midst of these thoughts, the office phone

started to ring. Instantly, he thought it was her, so he picked up quickly. Jennifer was on the outside of the glass wall that separated his office, and she could see that he was on the phone. His demeanor and everything seemed to shift when he got on the phone. It was not Rosanna. She knew this herself from a text that she had just received from Rosanna that read: "On my way now!"

Travon hung up the phone and gestured for Jennifer to come back in. She entered with good news.

"Rosanna just texted me and said she was on her way now," she said as she then showed him the message.

He maintained his composure but was pissed off inside that she would not answer his calls. She instead texted Jennifer even though he was the boss–and even more to her.

"Thank you, Jennifer, for being reliable. Now, where were we?"

"You wanted to have a meeting with the Vartan representatives to see if they were willing to part with the land they have uptown, so you can build townhouses on the property."

"Yes, please schedule a meeting with them. I'll come to them, and we can meet on the site—whatever appeases them. I want that property. If they settle for here, then have the restaurant on the first floor prepare a luncheon for them to enjoy while we take care of business," he said before he paused in thought, thinking about Rosanna's absence and behavior.

The phone call he received didn't help any. He'd had someone watching her for the last twenty-four hours since her behavior was kind of strange.

In the midst of his thoughts, she appeared and walked toward his office. She knocked on his door. He held up one finger to signify for her to wait before she entered.

"She's here now, Jennifer. I do appreciate your assistance and good work today. Follow up on that meeting and then get back to me."

"Yes, sir, I'm on it now," she said as she made her way out of the office and looked on at Rosanna trying to give her the heads-up about him not appreciating her not being around.

"Thank you for covering for me, Jennifer," Rosanna said as she passed her by.

"You're welcome, girl. He might be pissed," she said while continuing on with her daily duties and leaving Rosanna and Travon to deal with their problems.

"Good morning, Ms. Santos. Glad you could make it in today. Is everything okay with you and the home front?"

"Yes, yes. I just got a late start. That's all."

He leaned back in his chair and looked her in the eyes. He searched deeply for the truth because lies were being told right now, and he could not only hear it but he could feel it. Call it instinct.

"A late start? Is that all? Because I called you twice. A late start does not mean straight to voicemail."

"Wait a minute, you are my boss and, yes, the father of my son, but don't get it confused, because we are no longer together. So are we good with that?"

She flipped on him and quoted his own words from yesterday about mixing business with pleasure. He gave a light laugh before turning serious.

"You're right about the boss thing. So learn to speak in a lower tone and with respect. As for our son, my concern with you is primarily to assure that he was doing fine since we, you and I, are not in a relationship."

She looked at him and was angered by his words, yet nervous about all that was going on and him not seeing his son.

"Is there anything else you need to tell me?" he asked as a rhetorical question.

Sucking in a breath of stressed air she spoke with arrogance: "What do you mean by that?"

He gave her a look and stared deep into her eyes, a look she had never seen before backed by anger. It gave her the chills seeing the darkness in him. Her heart pounded and mind raced, knowing he was one for having many resources. *Does he know about Jamir? What about my friend that came to the house?* she thought.

"I don't have anything else to say. Then again I do," she said, thinking about what her son said about Disney World. "Why did you tell our son you're taking him to Disney World without telling me?"

"Because I plan on taking him—and not you. It's supposed to be a father-son moment."

"I still should be made aware of these things instead of our son telling me with excitement."

Hearing this made him feel good as a father. He was now looking forward to placing that smile on his son's face.

"We are going next week when I get back from the Vegas meeting with the investors from California. You don't have anything planned then, do you?" Then he said something that made her feel as if he already had the answer: "I can pick up our son from your mother's if you want me to, so you don't have to go get him. I know he was really excited about this trip," Travon said after giving her a flat look.

He didn't want her to see the gratification in his eyes or on his face. The call he received from his associate was about her mother coming to pick up his son, which meant she was at home doing something, because his son normally went to day care. So why send him to her mom's with a suitcase? He was also made aware of the gentleman that came to her place afterward.

Travon instructed the associate to find out more about the man who came to her place, and then get back to him as soon as possible. On the other hand, Rosanna was now in fear with the decision she was preparing to make. It would not work if he knew where their son was. She also didn't want to send out any red flags. But little did she know, it was too late for that! He was already alert and on to her while trying to figure out what was behind the smoke and mirrors.

"He told me to tell you he was at his grandmom's house and to come pick him up," she said with a tremulous tone. "He was probably making chocolate chip cookies with her," she said, stopping just as his phone rang.

Her eyes went to the phone as he answered it. She became quiet and tried to pick up on what was going on.

"My man, tell me something good," Travon said, listening to his associate on the other end. Rosanna nervously sat across from him looking into his eyes as he listened to the call. "Good, good! Get the pictures and whatever else you can produce, and then get back ASAP," he said before hanging up the phone and then walking around the glossy oak desk.

He started caressing Rosanna's hair. He then paused and grabbed the remote. He pressed the button which turned the clear glass walls to foggy white, which made it difficult to see through.

"Stand up," he said.

She obliged, since she didn't want to make matters worse since the day had started off wrong. She turned and faced him as he continued to caress her hair. He leaned in and kissed her forehead in between her eyebrows, which was her sensual spot.

"I do love you and I will always love you, because you brought my son into this world, but don't take that for granted," he said before he kissed her cheek and then her lips.

She didn't resist. Her arms wrapped around him as she buried her head into his chest as if to say *I'm sorry*. She really loved Travon, but he didn't want to settle down with her. She figured he wanted to have it all including his fun. Things would be different if she didn't have a son with him or have any feelings for him. Her decisions could be a lot easier as well as a lot less painful.

"If you want or need it, you can take some time off. Because when you're here, I need you to be at 100 percent."

She raised up her head and looked into his eyes.

"You're a very complex and mysterious man. I don't know how I let myself get twisted up emotionally with you, papi. The thing I don't regret between us is our son. He loves you just as much as I do. Only thing is, he has to have you and your time. Me, I get to be the sideshow and assistant."

"You're not the sideshow. I hold you at a higher level of respect than that," he started. "I think it would be good if you take a couple days off with pay."

She frowned her face up and felt even more distant from him as if he was pushing her away—all of the way out of the picture. *Before you know it, I'll be working at an office on the West Coast*, she thought.

"Whatever makes you happy! I just hope that punta you had dinner with last night is worth it all. Remember, no one can and will love you like I did. Just so you know and understand, it tears me apart to walk away from all of this without putting up a fight," she responded as she stormed out of the office and left him alone with his thoughts.

These deep thoughts fueled his paranoia even more. His greatest fear was growing old and being alone, and also growing old without people who genuinely loved him and not his money. He needed to figure out something so all that was going on around him and in his life would not turn out with him being alone in the end.

## Chapter 13

Two hours later, Travon was in his custom snow-white Audi R8 with chrome flakes in the paint that matched the chrome Asanti rims. This was the car he drove when he needed to clear his head by jumping onto the highway and opening up it, like he was doing now as he exited off I-81 and merged onto I-83 back to the city. He could see the I-83 bridge in his view as he weaved in and out of traffic while opening up the V-10 engine that pushed the car to 100 mph . . . 115 mph . . . 125 mph . . . 135 mph . . . 155 mph.

With the car going this fast, it dropped low and hugged the ground to prevent drag, which made the car go even faster yet smoothly. The car seemed to glide over the bridge before slowing down and passing the city exits when he came across the Hazelton exit back to I-81. He made his way over to his Forest Hills home listening to a mix by Large Flava, a known DJ in Harrisburg.

Travon was having many thoughts about Rosanna, his son, his business partners and the empire they had built, and Sarah, a woman that was capable of capturing his attention physically, mentally, and emotionally. He didn't understand how, especially being one never to take any women seriously in order to avoid attachment and heartbreak. However, there was something about her that made him gravitate toward her. He wanted more of her good sex, and he wanted to get to know who she really was and what she had to offer him from a relationship standpoint. She was his newness, his breath of fresh air, and a much-needed change to his life. He thought about her and now had feelings for her.

Before entering into his estate, he turned down the music. He didn't want it to blare in his quiet suburban area. As he pulled into the cul de sac, he could see Ms. Connie Peterson walking her German shepherd. The dog gave her a sense of protection when her husband was not around. Travon beeped his horn at her before rolling down his window to speak like a gentleman.

"How are you doing today?"

She halted in her tracks when she saw who it was, especially having a thing for him.

"Hi, Travon, I'm doing fine. Just trying to walk the dog and stay in shape at the same time. You?"

He laughed as she placed her hand on her hip trying to be sexy in her pink Prada sweat suit. Her dog, Dallas, wore a Luis Vuitton collar and leash.

"Don't let the dog walk you," he said as he pulled off into his driveway.

He noticed a white Yukon Denali parked in Sarah's driveway. He smiled while thinking how the country girl went and purchased a truck instead of a car that would compliment her sexy natural look and house.

He stepped out of his car all ready to make his way over to Sarah's house to get his dose of happiness, when he caught movement out of the corner of his eye. Somebody was in his house.

His heart started to race as he rushed toward the front door. He also quickly pulled out his legal and licensed nickel-plated Colt 10 mm with a pearl handle.

As he was unlocking the door, Sarah called out to him, "Hey, you!"

He didn't have time for that right now. He didn't even look her way. He was too focused on seeing who the hell was in his house.

"Hey, sexy," she called out again as he entered the house with his gun out in front with his finger on the trigger.

He shut the door behind him and swept from side to side. He then flipped off the safety with his thumb. *Who the hell is in my house and why?* he asked himself as he took steps through the house where he had seen someone move. This had never happened to him before. His heart began to beat at a rapid pace while his mind thought of the worst outcome with an intruder in his home. Many different scenarios raced through his mind as he took each step, yet each of the scenarios ended with him killing whoever was in his home.

He swung into the kitchen and saw the blinds on the back door move, which signified that it had been used in the last few seconds. He instantly rushed over to the door and turned the knob. *It's locked, but it can't be!* he thought as he turned quickly and rushed up the steps to check each room. Nothing! Nothing. There was no one in the house.

"I know I'm not seeing things?" he said aloud, closing his eyes and taking a deep breath.

In that same instance, he could see a glimpse of the person inside his house. The glimpse was from the angle he originally spotted the movement out of the corner of his eye. Something was not right, he thought as he scanned around the room. Nothing seemed disturbed. With him being a perfectionist, he would detect anything out of place.

He made his way back down to the ADT security key pad, and there were numbers on the digital screen. It showed nine random numbers, but they were not the code to his alarm system nor were they the numbers he had punched in. However, at least now he had mentally locked the numbers into his brain before clearing them off the screen and arming the system. He exited the home and walked outside to the driveway, and stared at all of the houses then back to his own. A feeling came over him again raising his paranoia to another level. He knew he lived a secret and mysterious life and lifestyle; however, living this way allowed him to succeed thus far.

His focus shifted toward Sarah's driveway when he heard a truck start up. But it was not Sarah he saw in the driver's seat. It was a man he had never seen before. His mind and emotions were mixed as he tried to process what he was seeing, thinking, and feeling, especially after seeing the man wave to Sarah as he backed out of the driveway. She was standing there with short shorts on and a white T-shirt tied up to expose her flat stomach. Her hair was wet and down from a shower. The wet hair didn't help his thoughts or emotions.

"Are you going to come over here and speak to me, or was last night enough for you?" she yelled out after seeing Travon staring at her and her guest.

He really didn't know what to think about what he was seeing.

He put his gun back into the car before making his way over to her while he still processed what had just taken place. At the same time, he eyed down the driver of the Yukon, but the driver didn't look his way at all as if he was afraid to make eye contact—another red flag.

"You seemed to be in a hurry when I called you the first time. What's eating at you?" she asked while coming closer and placing her hand on his chest.

Any other time he would enjoy her touch, but he removed her hand since he was so caught up in his thoughts.

"Somebody was in my house as I was pulling in."

"Oh my! I guess my calling you at the same time didn't help any or make you feel any better about it. You should call the cops."

"No need, since nothing is out of place," he said while looking into her eyes. "So, who's your friend?"

"One of those sales people trying to get me to buy some furniture direct from the factory for half price," she said while extending her hands, placing one softly and gently on his arm and the other lightly on his chest.

"You want to come in and get whatever it is off your mind? You can talk to me. I want you to know that I'm more than sex and a pretty face."

A smile came across his face upon hearing her words that reached down into his heart, even through he was still angry about an intruder being in his home. But why? He glanced at his platinum Rolex, and she caught it and noted that he was one for being punctual.

"Checking the time? Don't want to miss any meetings or business engagements."

"Yes, because I have an hour or so before I have to be somewhere," he responded as they made their way into her house.

Connie was being nosey and looking on with her dog. She envied Sarah's charming ability to get close to Travon. Sarah instinctively turned and made eye contact with Connie and batted her eyes at her while smiling. The two of them entered the house, which left Connie to assume what they were going to do next.

## Chapter 14

"Travon, you want anything to drink: wine, cognac, juice, water, or soda?" Sarah asked him, offering up some hospitality.

"Water will be just fine. Remember, I have to get back to work," he responded, sitting on the bench in the foyer. She made her way into the kitchen and got him a bottled water and herself a glass of wine.

Travon took a few minutes to himself and looked around. He remained in deep thought while playing everything back in his mind. He knew he needed to be safe and protect himself and all of his worth. His son could have easily been in the house when the intruder came. Not good. He didn't even like the thought of this, and it angered him even more. He really wanted to catch the person that was in his house fumbling around with his security keypad and leaving those numbers in. *Could the numbers explain how they bypassed my system? If so who wanted to get in that bad, and why did they not take anything?* So many thoughts entered his mind.

Sarah came back in with a bottled water in her hand for him while she sipped from her glass of wine.

"Here you go, sweetness," she said as she handed him the bottle of water and then sat down beside him. "Tell me, what's on your mind? I'm a good listener, you know," she said while leaning back against his shoulder.

He could feel the affection in her presence, which made her stand out even more emotionally to him.

"Trust is everything. When we lack trust, we become paranoid to open up emotionally or in business. It's human nature in our ability to sense fear or danger."

She sat up straight wanting to look him in the eyes as she spoke. She held her wine glass in one hand while caressing his shoulder with her other.

"Can you trust me to be more than a friend to you? To be your comfort zone and the one who really gets and understands you?" she asked as she took a sip of her wine.

A brief silence fell, which allowed him to process her question as well as his answer.

"Trust takes time; however, when it comes to you, I like and appreciate the path we're on. So don't give me any reason not to build a bond of trust with you," he said as he placed his hand over hers on his shoulder.

"So who is it you suddenly don't trust? I ask because I know it's not me, so it must be someone at the office."

"A few people I have close to me. Even those that know me best, which is the worst feeling when losing faith and trust in those you invest in."

"You need to distance yourself from them before they tear you down and make you into a bad man. That will lead you to make bad decisions and place you in a bad position far from all that you have and want right now," she said while caressing his arm now along with his mind and heart, when he heard her words flow deep into his heart and mind.

"Travon, most men aren't big on titles and giving things labels; however, I want to be with you. I want to be yours. Not just because the sex is mind-blowing and my body wants more of yours, but because I believe we'll become one another's daily desire with time and trust, and every day we'll find new reasons why we want it to keep going."

His eyes locked on hers as the words flowed from her mouth and connected with him. He leaned in and kissed her soft lips, which tasted like the red wine she was drinking. Her heart was happy in this moment, and his heart felt the same. His wall of protection was slowly coming down and giving her what she had yearned for.

"I'm going to be good to you, Sarah, as long as you give me 100 percent. No lies! No games! No secrets."

He then paused and placed more kisses to her soft sweet lips, filled with passion and creating an emotional explosion inside of their hearts, which made them feel every ounce of the intimate kiss.

"I'll be good to you, too, Travon. I really want your trust and your all to make this so special, and I promise my heart, mind, and body will be good to you," she said, sounding sincere and sexual all at once.

"Time will tell how this will all play out. So if you stick around and have the time, good things will continue to take place for your heart, mind, and body," he said, literally mirroring her words.

She wanted more while looking into his eyes and hearing his words. She also wanted a future, because she loved the vision she was having of him trusting her and believing every word she said. It was both good love and the good life. She closed her eyes and leaned into his lips, kissing with the passion that was racing through her heart and body as her hands roamed over his body. His hands found her curves of perfection, which were soft and sensual. She wanted him just as she had last night. He wanted more of her warm, wet, tight love spot that felt just right. In between the passionate kissing and heavy petting, their clothes came off over their bodies until they stood bare on the cool marble floor. They lay on it, only adding to the sensation as their bodies heated up with erotic fire and a burning desire to be appeased.

His lips slid over her breasts, which stimulated her in every way and made her body become sensitive. His lips kissed in between her breasts and then to her side, before kissing around her belly button and then going lower and lower. She squirmed while feeling her body purr ready for what was next. His hands parted her legs as his lips gently came face-to-face with her pretty kitty, where he placed a light kiss.

"Mmmmh!" she moaned, placing her hands on his head and caressing his soft hair just as his tongue began its magic swirling on her pearl with intense speed almost like a vibrating sensation. This sent waves of pleasure through her body and made her moan as the feeling of pleasure took over her body.

"Aaaah, aaaah, aaaah, Trae," she let out, now feeling his thick fingers assist his tongue magic as he thrust two fingers into her tight, wet love while he stimulated her heart and body with each pulsating thrust that pleased her.

His tongue went faster as his lips covered the pearl containing it from getting away as it slid over his tongue over and over. The erotic sensations surged through her as the feelings of butterflies in her stomach full of sexual excitement and the feeling of an orgasm rushed through her body.

"Haaaa, haaaa, aaaaah, aaaah! Ooooohhhh,

Trae, Trae! Mmmmmmh! Mmmmmh! Oh, Trae! What is happening to my body? Mmmmmmh! Oh God, Oh God! Mmmmmmmmh!"

Her moaning added to the erotic tongue play, allowing him to know he was discovering her body one swirl of the tongue at a time, backed by his fingers working their angle and thrusting deep into her love spot. It made her wetter, hornier, and even more orgasmic.

She could feel her stomach tightening, her heart fluttering, and her mind racing as this powerful pulsating pleasure of passion was passing through her body like a wave of sensation the faster his tongue moved and the harder his finger thrust into her wet, tight pussy.

"Ohhhhh, God! Mmmmmmmmh! Mmmmmmmh! Aaaaaaah, aaaah, aaaah, aaaah!"

More intense moaning took place as her orgasmic ball of fire was reaching its peak ready to explode, ready to be released from her body, and ready to cum all over his tongue and fingers to show them that they were doing a great job. She could not hold back any more. *Here it comes. It's coming fast.*

"Ohhhh, Trae, Trae, Trae! Mmmmmmmmh! Mmmmmmh! Aaaah, aaaah, aaaaah, aaaaah, aaaaah!" she let out in between breathing heavy and hot air.

She tried to embrace the orgasmic eruption that was exploding and racing from her body and stimulating her heart, mind, and body. She never had this feeling before and never had someone please her pretty kitty like this ever in her life. Men where she lived didn't do this. They were all into slam, bam, thank you, ma'am, sex. But this right here was tongue love-making to her body.

"Ooooh, oooooh, oooooh, oooooh!" she continued moaning as her juices flowed from her body over his tongue, which tasted sweet to him and made his tongue slide over her pearl even more as he pushed his fingers deep from side to side, in and out of her soaking wet love spot.

Then he took his fingers out, only to place his tongue inside of her. He began to go fast—in and out, in and out, in and out—with sexual speed that added even more erotic pleasure to the feeling she was already having. Her legs were now shaking as his tongue thrust in and out, in and out, in and out. His fingertips massaged her pearl, which added a strong sensation and made her stomach clench continuously as she was having multiple orgasms. This was another first for her that blew her mind yet captured her heart.

"Ahhhh, ahhhhh, ahhhh, aaaaaah, aaaaah, aaaaah, aaaaah, mmmmmmmh! Mmmmmmh!" she moaned as her heart, mind, and body took this orgasmic ride of a lifetime and made her feel so good as she was squirting her cum all over his tongue and fingers.

He loved the taste and the flow of her love juices.

"Yesssss! Mmmmmmmh! Mmmmmmmmh! Oh God, Oh God!"

The orgasmic eruptions to her seemed endless, but she didn't complain. She loved the feeling that stimulated her vision to see a promising future with him filled with love. So many good thoughts came to her as he was working his tongue magic. Then she came back down off of the high orgasmic horse when he stopped his tongue play with her pretty kitty. Her eyes opened as he came back up toward her while her body was still trembling like an orgasm aftershock. He could see the emotions in her eyes sparkling back at him. Her eyes smiled, and her heart and body were happy as well, loving his touch, his look, and his body. Even more, she loved the vision of a promising future she had with him. A tear of happiness that was backed by the multiple orgasms slid down the side of her face. Upon seeing this, Travon leaned in kissing it away.

"Everything is going to be okay. I'm not going anywhere, nor do I plan on playing with you or your feelings," he whispered into her ear.

She wrapped her legs and arms around him.

"Make love to me and my body forever," she said in the most sexy Southern accent that charmed its way into his ears, heart, and mind as he obliged her intimate request.

This time, however, he entered slow with deep strokes as he whispered sweet love into her ear, making her heart connect to every stroke and promise he was making to her.

"This is the beginning of true romance with you. We're going to have the world at our fingertips, so our focus is going to be each other and me making your heart happy at all times," he whispered with his lips up close to her ear, adding sensation to this intimate sexual session. "I promise to be good to you and listen to you and your heart through good or bad times. I'll be there for you," he added, before going deep and hard yet slow to make love to her body. Light moans flowed from her mouth upon feeling his thickness, and his length made her pretty kitty purr.

"Trae, you make me feel so good! Mmmmmmh! Mmmmmmh! Mmmmmh! I don't want this to ever end. Mmmmmmmh! Yesss, mmmmmmmh!" she moaned again, feeling the pulsating power of orgasms coming through her body again with each long, deep stroke.

His pace picked up now, and he felt himself

about to cum. His speed and deep strokes also made her feel like she was cumming, too.

"I want to cum when you cum," he whispered into her ear as he was going harder, deeper, and faster while feeling the uncontrollable power race through his long, thick love stick that erupted inside of her as he was slamming the remaining strokes deep into her love kitty.

"Don't move, Trae! Mmmmmmmh! Mmmmmmh! I, I, I'm cumming again. Mmmmmmmmh aaaaah, aaaaaah!" she moaned, feeling the eruption take over her body. "Thank you. Mmmmmmmmh! Yessss, mmmmmmmh! Thank you, mmmmmmmmh! Damn, you're so special! Mmmmmmmmh!" she let out before placing a love bite to his shoulder while trying to embrace the orgasm that was taking over her mind, heart, and body.

Her biting into his shoulder turned him on and made him rise up again stiffening to be put to work again. She could feel him growing inside of her, but he could not continue. He needed to get to his meeting. He wished he could stay, but he had to go.

"Sarah, baby, I really have to be at this meeting. I want to do this all night and day, but it's important I get to this meeting," he told her.

"Well, you have to freshen up before you go. I

don't want my love juices on your lips when you roll into the meeting," she said, getting a smile out of him. "So get in the shower with me, and then you can head to your business meeting. Me and my pretty kitty, along with my heart, will be here waiting on you."

"Let's take a shower without getting side-tracked."

"I won't, but will you?" she said, squeezing her kitty on his thickness and giving him a smile with eyes of seduction.

"Damn, you're good, but I really got to go!" he said, pulling out of her while still stiff. "Where's the shower?"

"Follow me," she said as they walked away looking like art in motion the way she strutted her naked beauty.

He followed behind her and headed up to take a shower. All he could think about was how good she was with her Southern allure. She was definitely one that stood out in every respect.

## Chapter 15

Four months had passed by, and business was going well for the Global Image Group. The casino and resort in Las Vegas were underway. They were also working on getting a license to put slots and some blackjack tables in their Red Scorpion nightclubs as well as the new one they just built on the City Island, which was a perfect location for the city of Harrisburg and the towns connected by the bridges that led to the island along the Susquehanna River. Global Image Group was all about expanding, which would allow them to increase employment wherever they built or opened up.

For Travon and Sarah, life was good, and their love got better by the day. They kept everything as new and exciting as the first day and time they met and became intimate. Their future was looking bright thus far. Finally, he had allowed himself to open up to see the other side of a relationship with one woman when both parties were giving their all mentally, physically, emotionally, and financially.

There was no more side rendezvousing with Melissa at the club as much as she craved his body, touch, and good love stick. He didn't give in because he was falling each day for Sarah. In the beginning Melissa was upset, but she soon became captivated by this new Travon. She wished she could have been to him what Sarah was. She admired Sarah, because her presence alone made Travon a different man—a man most women could only dream about. Melissa also made Travon aware of how lucky Sarah was to have captured all of his attention.

Rosanna didn't share the same views or respect for Sarah as did Melissa and the other women at the office. In her eyes, Sarah had stolen him away from her and their son. Sarah came into the picture with one thing on her mind; however, she got more than she expected. She learned so much more about him, the more he trusted her and opened up to her. He made her feel welcome into his heart and life since he was an open book with no secrets. She also became an open book and made him aware of things she didn't plan on telling him at first.

She didn't know she was going to fall for him as she had done thus far. She had heard about this happening to other women, but love—like the real love that was in her heart—was the feeling she got when Travon was in the room or simply looked at her without words. She could feel it in her body that he loved her too.

The most interesting thing about the two of them falling in love, and each of them sharing the same powerful emotions, was that neither of them used the word *love* or the phrase *I love you*. However, their hearts and minds knew the truth.

Travon allowed Rosanna to seek another job since she could not bear to be around Sarah or him after she realized they had become a real couple. Rosanna secured a lucrative position with Legacy Car Rentals that was started in 2004 by Tom Jones. His businesses were now nationwide with luxury rental offices.

The only time Travon and Rosanna spoke was when he would come around to see his son or pick him up for the weekend. However, each time it brought back memories that forced her emotional pain to arise.

Travon now prepared to make a life-changing decision to surprise Sarah. She was at home getting dressed for a date with her man, when the black-and-gray Maybach pulled up in front of her place. She came out ready to see what her man had in store for her. As she exited, she saw the tall African American formally and professionally dressed in black.

"Good morning, ma'am," he said after opening the door so she could take a seat on the plush leather.

Sarah was wearing three-inch Roberto Cavali heels, white YSL jeans with gold stitching that flowed with her Vera Wang silk blouse with gold print, and a clutch by D&G that added to her freshly manicured nails and styled hair. She looked sexy and elegant, and she smelled even more alluring wearing Gucci's Guilty Pleasure perfume. The driver closed the door as she gracefully entered. Then he got in, and they took off to the destination to where he was directed.

There was a card inside the Maybach beside a picture of her and Travon at the Farm Show Complex on Cameron Street in the city. She was holding two baby chickens in the photo. The picture allowed her to reflect back to the moment she shared with him that day as well as the laughter and the different foods they ate. Travon even got out of his comfort zone standing in the mud with the pigs and sheep. The thought of that day made her smile, because she knew he would do anything to make her feel comfortable and happy.

She opened the card that read: "With you I see the world a lot more clear. With you I am a better person: passionate, yet permeating with affection and happiness. With you, my day begins knowing you have my best interest and my heart, because we're more than friends."

As she read the card, she covered her mouth. She got a love feeling as her heart beat and her mind raced mind. Thoughts filled her head and made her somewhat scared. The scared feeling was what true love feels like. If fear didn't enter the equation, then they would both be living a life of deception. Love feels so good that at times it's scary, because it does not happen all the time. Sarah's heart came to a calm after feeling herself get overemotional as she gravitated toward Travon and his heart by just reading the words that he had taken the time to express and write down.

"Ma'am, are you okay back there?" the driver questioned after seeing her cover her mouth with a look of wow that was backed by tears of happiness.

"Tears of joy and happiness, that's all. Thank you for asking," she said while wiping away the tears as she looked out the window wondering to herself.

She questioned what she had gotten herself into. It was a good that felt good, but somehow bad images kept occurring. Could they be from her past? Or was it a fear she was having of someone truly wanting to love and support her to the fullest?

She hit the switch on the curtains and closed them on the back windows to conceal her from the outside. This gave her some alone time to think about the man she loved and was falling in love with, even though she never told him that she loved him or that she was head over heels for him and the love he had inside for her. Without question, she displayed this affection of love to him on a daily basis. So many thoughts and emotions went through her mind and heart right now, but everything came to a pause as her phone rang and cut into what she was thinking. It brought her back to the moment at hand.

She saw the name of the caller trying to reach her. It was not Travon; and in this moment, he was all that mattered. So she tapped Ignore and sent the call to voicemail. Then she turned the phone all the way off, since the person she was going to be with was the only one she needed to speak with.

The Maybach drove onto the Harrisburg International Airport property where Travon was waiting in his private G4 jet that was outfitted with all of the amenities of a successful millionaire.

"We're here, ma'am," the driver said as he stepped out and opened the door by the red carpet that led to the inside of the jet. "Enjoy your trip, ma'am."

"Trip! Oh my, he is full of surprises," Sarah said as she made her way up the steps and then looked around to embrace this affluent lifestyle. As she stepped inside the plane, she saw Travon standing there with a bottle of Peach CÎROC and two shot glasses. He was already two shots in waiting on her arrival.

"This is so unexpected but impressive," she said with her charming accent as she came over to kiss him.

"I have a surprise for you. Besides, trips like this keep the excitement going in a relationship. I want to keep your heart, mind, and body happy at all times. It's my way of showing you that you are appreciated, and that what we have together is more than good times under the sheets. Now, pretty lady, take a seat and enjoy this bottle with me. We'll be in flight for a few hours."

She was smiling inside and out while embracing the moment with the good man before her. She sat across from him, which allowed her to take in all of his good looks. At the same time, it allowed her to appreciate what she had in him.

He poured her a triple shot so she could catch up to him. She drank half of it before licking her lips and savoring the flavor over her tongue.

"So, I take it our destination is private, too?"

"A private island in the Bahamas with priceless and intimate views," he said with a smile before taking another drink. "We'll be by ourselves so we can run around naked, if you like?"

"Let me think about it. I guess if I drink a few more of these, I'd run a marathon in my birthday suit as long as I have you to chase after me," she said, which made him laugh.

They then both tilted back their shot glasses and emptied them, so he refilled both glasses.

"Come over here with me. We're about to take off," he said, feeling the jet lining up for the runway.

The G4 was outfitted with custom push-button seats that reclined and declined at the client's choice. He hit the button that allowed the seats to go back just a little, which let her snuggle up next to him as they continued to drink and talk.

"Travon, for good or bad, I never want the good in you to end. I really like you and appreciate how you treat me," she said after placing a kiss on his cheek. "I think you and I stumbled onto something unique, and it feels so good inside to me."

She lovingly caressed his neck with her manicured nails. It was a sensual sensation that allowed him to feel her affection through her intimate touch and words.

"Let's have one more drink and then we can watch a movie," he said before pouring the two of them another shot.

He then grabbed the remote and turned on the 42-inch flat wide-screen, and a movie came on that put a smile on Sarah's face.

This is my favorite movie!"

"It's my job as your man to know what you like,

love, dislike, and hate. I remember in one conversation that you mentioned how this was your favorite, because she gets her happy ending and her knight in shining armor," he said.

He then pressed another button that closed the shades on the widows to make it dark. He also dimmed the lights. The movie he selected was *Pretty Woman,* featuring Julia Roberts and Richard Gear.

She continued caressing his neck as they watched the movie. The time they had shared made both of them feel a close emotional bond. He placed his arm around her and kissed her soft lip. He could feel the love, passion, and excitement of the relationship. He wanted more with her, and he also wanted her to know that he was not going anywhere until she no longer desired all that he had to offer. So until then, he planned on giving her all of him—the world of emotions and happiness. As these thoughts came to him, he glanced over and watched her enjoying the movie. This was love!

## Chapter 16

A few hours had passed, with the private jet flying toward the Bahamian island. The pilot woke up Travon as the plane began descending toward the runway that was lined on both sides with palm trees and tropical blue waters.

"This is so beautiful," Sarah said as the plane continued its descent.

"This is just a glimpse of what you'll see," he said, kissing her cheek and loving her innocence of never being out of the country before as she had once told him.

He kept this information in the back of his mind, because he wanted to make her dreams come true of going abroad one day.

The plane landed and the tires screeched when they made contact with the black-topped runway. It didn't take long before it came to a full stop. As the stairs came down for their exit from the plane, they were greeted by a limo awaiting them. Travon had planned everything from start to finish. He didn't want anything to be out of line of the way he had envisioned it. The limo took them to the docks where a sixty-foot Bayliner awaited to take them to the private island that Travon had rented out for him and his woman.

It didn't take long before the boat closed in on the private island and gave Sarah a true visual of art in the picturesque scene. As they approached, no one could miss the twenty thousand-square-foot main house with two floors at the top of the island. It was surrounded by employee huts, a spa with a sauna, a Jacuzzi, and a staff ready to give massages and more. The home also boasted floor-to-ceiling glass walls that allowed the guests to view the island and all its creations from every angle.

She also saw horse stalls with white horses, and a yacht with a speed boat and Jet Skis off to the side. This place was a millionaire's playground, and Sarah just so happened to be in love with a millionaire who was willing to give her the world. At the same time, he would show her the world as they built on their relationship and made memories along the way, even with the things he had planned today.

The white sands and blue waters allowed her to experience paradise as she had seen it in magazines and on TV.

The staff on the island walked up and handed her a piña colada and strawberry daiquiri along with ice-cold shots of Belvedere for Travon.

"Welcome to Hidden Treasures, a private island. Anything you need or can think of, we're at your service. All of your primary requests you sent have been taken care of as you desired," the Bahamian woman said as she handed each of them their designated drink.

The frozen piña colada was handed to Sarah first, because she had once mentioned to Travon that the drink was the closest she'd ever gotten to a tropical island, and he listened. The daiquiri was also given to her, so she could select which drink she wanted. Travon took both shots of vodka and slammed them down back to back. He then took her hand that didn't have the drink in it, and escorted her to the main house.

"Travon, hold on, let me take off my heels," Sarah said, slipping them off.

He then took them from her, held them in his right hand, and then continued to lead her with his left. The white sand felt good on her bare feet.

"You know, as a country girl, I've never been to a beach or an island. The only beauty like this I've ever seen has been on television. I like the way the sand feels on my feet."

"You know, I saw something far more beautiful than this island the moment I set eyes on you," he said, which made her smile ear to ear as she sipped on her drink.

She could feel every word he was saying because it was backed up by the truth.

"Kiss me, baby!" she said, wanting more of his affection.

He leaned in and kissed her soft wet lips,

which tasted of coconut and pineapple.

"Now, let's go to the house to see what they have for us," he said, loving how he was feeling—and more importantly, how she was feeling.

Three staff members stood in front of the house as they walked up, and each of them had a welcoming smile.

"Welcome, Mr. Robinson and Ms. Duvall. We are here to cater to your every desire. As requested, Ms. Sarah, we have plenty of clothes for you to choose from all in your size, including your shoe size, which is a six and a half, correct?"

"Yes, how did he know that?" Sarah asked Travon.

"Because I listen. I observe the woman I'm with to make sure I can give her the things she needs, even if she does not know she needs them until they appear," Travon said, which placed another smile on her face.

Travon had sent forms with all of their likes and dislikes from clothing to food to adventures.

"Since you told them all the things I want, like, and desire, did you tell them I only want you? Can they serve you up with a bucket of ice so I can let it melt all over that sexy body in between kisses," she said with a smile. "Oh, with chocolate-covered strawberries, too, for added sweetness and passion."

"Would that be white or dark chocolate, Ms. Duvall?" the Bahamian male server asked.

She started to laugh and was a bit in shock by the staff's prompt service, even though she was just being funny and messing around with her man. But their job was to please the clients. There was no request within reason that they would not attempt to appease.

"Both! Thank you. He likes the white and I love the dark chocolate," Sarah said, still being funny.

This time the male staff member got what she was saying, so he laughed as well. Her comment that she loved chocolate resonated with Travon's ears and heart, because they still had not told one another that they loved each other. However, the feeling was there, and it was getting deeper with each second they were together bonding, making memories, and sharing special times like this.

They made their way into the sumptuous home with designer furniture imported from around the world. Most of the decor paid respect to the Bahamian culture and heritage. There were white marble floors with traces of 24-karat gold throughout them. All of it matched the gold statues, white couches with gold pillows, and paintings that cost upward of a million dollars each for the millionaires and billionaires that visited the island to view and appreciate. The floor-to-ceiling windows were art in themselves, and they allowed visitors to capture the picturesque images from every direction.

"Mr. Robinson, we have food cooking on the grill out back on the deck," the female server announced.

"Good, because Sarah had me drinking on the flight, so I'm hungry now," Travon joked.

Sarah nudged him with her bare foot, before they made their way to the back side of the house. As soon as they opened the sliding back doors, they could smell the island food in the air, which made them even hungrier. Once they stepped outside, they saw all the food on the grill being cooked by the chef: shrimp, whole corn, salmon, jerk chicken, lamb, and conch—all foods from the island along with sides and more alcohol.

They were seated and served, which allowed them to indulge in the good food and conversation as they listened to the ocean waves crash up onto the beach. Sarah was thinking that she could definitely get used to this lifestyle and not return to the life she was living before she had met him. His love, good sex, and the way he treated a woman like she deserved to be treated would change anyone's mind from their original plans.

They filled up on food before they headed down to the beach area where the staff had already set up lounge beach chairs and towels embroidered with their names, of which Sarah took notice. She really admired the detail that had been put into everything thus far.

A bottle of apple martinis was on ice for her while they had prepared a bottle of pre-mixed Long Islands for Travon. Assorted flowers circled the towels in the shape of a heart.

Travon held her hand and looked on at the spread of perfection set up by the staff.

“I cannot believe they have my name on the towel. I’m definitely keeping it when we leave,” she said, making him laugh, even though she was really serious because it was a part of the memory she would always have of him.

“There will be more towels and even more memories to share with me as long as you believe in me and what we’re going to have,” he said before taking off his shirt and tossing his pants to the side along with his shoes.

“I see you’re wearing the Tommy Hilfiger boxers I bought you. Must say they look so sexy on you, and I cannot wait to get them off of you,” she said, placing a kiss to his chest. “Can we stay here forever and never go back to the States?”

She really meant every word about not wanting to go back to Pennsylvania, because she wanted to live this life of luxury that all women fantasized about. He kissed her forehead with love. He just wanted to please her and wished he could just stay here forever with her.

"Anything is possible if you want it and believe in it enough. Truthfully, this would be the perfect life to live and be with that special one you would always appreciate," he said, which melted her heart. "Now, let's me and you relax and take in the beauty of this sunset."

She slipped out of her clothes into a powder-blue lace panty-and-bra set from the Victoria's Secret Angel's collection.

"You look good, Sarah. I appreciate what I see. More importantly, I enjoy the feelings I get when we're together or the thoughts I have of you when you're not around. That always puts me in a good mood," he said while opening the apple martini for her and pouring a glass of Long Island Iced Tea for himself. She sat with her glass in hand and stared at him as he spoke. She really only wanted him to say the three little words, so she could reply, "Me too."

They drank and enjoyed the conversation and the emotional passion. They bonded and felt the strong connection with each word expressed from their hearts. They found one another's lips and kissed with the same love that their lips had yet to speak. However, the fireworks in this kiss of passion gave their hearts the exploding fire of intimacy, and then as they parted from the kiss, each of them seemed to feel it deep in their emotional core.

Travon's eyes locked in on Sarah's as he was savoring the sweetness of her lips on his.

"I love you, Sarah."

Hearing these words instantly sent butterflies into her heart as this euphoric stimulation of the heart and mind made her feel light and warm. It was the high of the feeling and the confirmation that he felt the same as her. The smile on her heart and face said it all.

"I love you too, Travon."

He embraced her words as he pointed to the picturesque sunset.

"Look at how beautiful it is," he said, shifting her attention.

The sun was dusting the sky with reds, oranges, and powder blues that were all fading to a slow darkness.

"I never experienced something so amazing and breathtaking," Sarah said while taking in the full view of Mother Nature's artwork.

"It has nothing on this," he said, placing a kiss on her lips before pulling back.

He then brought into view a four-carat solitaire Ashoka diamond set in platinum. It was flawless in color, cut, and clarity, and it sparkled under the sunset. It was worth the quarter million dollars and change that he had paid for it to express his love and commitment to her.

Once Sarah saw it, it took away her breath as her heart felt like it was being hugged by his love.

“Oh my Lord! Is this what I think it is?” she questioned, with eyes still locked on the sparkling diamond.

“Yes, it is! What do you think it is? I bought this with you in mind and in my heart. Now that we have that understood, I want to ask you if you can be more than a girlfriend to me. I love you, and I want to hold on to you and what we have forever until my last breath. So will you marry me, and make me the luckiest man in the world?”

Her eyes filled with tears of joy, both mentally and emotionally. She was so overwhelmed yet excited about this love story. She put her hands over her mouth and shook with the love that was running through her heart and body, along with a million thoughts.

“Yes, yes! I will marry you! I love you, Travon! I really do love you, no matter what! I appreciate everything you do for me and our relationship,” she expressed, extending her left hand while still shaking.

Tears streamed down her face, but they were

all backed up by love and joy in her heart, mind, and body. It was the day most women yearn to see and experience.

"I promise to always be good to you and your heart, mind, and body, no matter what," he said, kissing her hand before he put the ring on. His kissing continued up her arm, then her shoulder, over to her neck, and then her ear. "I'm going to cherish and appreciate every part of your body until my last breath," he whispered into her ear before kissing her cheek and then her soft sweet lips.

Her arms came around and embraced him. They lay on the large beach towels osculating with passion.

"Make love to me forever, Trae," she let out emotionally into the night of love and passion.

She took control and pushed him over onto his back. She then kissed his chest and massaged him with her loving touch. The kisses trailed down to his tight stomach. She could feel his love stick rise up and press hard against her breasts in her lace bra. She slid his boxer shorts off and kissed his legs. Her soft hands took hold of him, followed by her soft, wet, and warm lips sucking on him with vibrant pleasure. His breathing changed the more her soft hands and wet warm lips slid up and down on his thick long love stick. She could feel his thickness pulsate as the veins in his dick throbbed in her soft grip.

"Damn, baby! This feels good," he let out while breathing heavily as she was humming on him.

She then paused and licked her lips. She blew him a kiss as she slipped out of her panties and then bra. She climbed on top of him and mounted his long thickness that made her pretty kitty purr and fill her tight wet love spot that was pulsating. She wanted to be pleased by all of him physically and emotionally in this love-making session.

"Mmmmnmh! I love you, Trae! Mmmmmh!"

"I love you, too, country girl. Your wet love feels so good to me," he said while cupping her soft ass and helping her to ride him up and down, up and down, slow, deep, and hard, just as her kitty liked it.

It was even better slow because it felt like her heart was also being made love to under the stars that covered the night sky.

"Aaaaaah, aaaaah, Trae! Mmmmmmmmh!" she moaned as she leaned into his love stick.

She could feel it deep inside of her, which sent a rush of pleasure through her body. At the same time, she pressed her manicured nails into his chest and looked into his eyes. She was making love to him as much as he was making love to her, especially tonight being his fiancée.

"I'm so loving this, baby. Damn, damn! You feel so good! Oh yeah, work it!" he said as her hips shifted motion and allowed his length and thickness to hit every part of her insides, which stimulated her heart and body and stirred up the sensation that was building up by the second.

Her nails in his chest turned him on even more and made him thrust deep into her love while he squeezed her ass at the same time. His masculine grip on her soft ass only added to the intense pleasure she was feeling as her body filled with butterflies that were stirring inside of her.

Looking into his eyes, she could tell he was ready to cum. She could also feel his long thickness tighten up. This feeling triggered a surge of pleasure that rushed through her body as she started riding him harder, going up and down on his long thickness, with her hips and ass going up and down while still looking into his eyes and moaning.

"Aaaaah, yes, Trae! Mmmmmmmmh! I want to cum when you come, Trae," she said, going faster and riding him harder and harder while feeling this whirlwind of orgasmic pulsating pleasure she could no longer hold back inside her.

It was racing through her body and stimulating her heart and mind, ready to be released. She could not hold back any longer.

"Ohhhh, ohhhhhh God! Mmmmmmmmh, mmmmmmh! I love you, Trae! Mmmmmmmmh."

The wave of orgasms erupted from her body over and over. She rode him faster, up and down, up and down.

"I'm cumming, too, baby. Damn, oh shit! This feels so damn good. I love you, baby!" he let out.

His grip was still tight on her ass, which enhanced the sensation that she felt and even more so when he exploded inside of her. She leaned in and slowed down her ride, but she still moved her hips.

"I, I, I'm cumming with you, Trae! Mmnmmmmh! Mmmmmh! Yes, I love you! Mmmmmmmmh!" she said, moaning into his ear and leaning on him.

She could now feel his love fluid erupting inside of her. Being his fiancée, she now was ready to have his baby and make a family with him, so feeling his eruption only added to her love for him and pleasure in her body. This love session was more than sex. It was emotional bonding and making memories all at once. It would be a night they would never forget. Her love bites to his neck and shoulder turned him on even more. Her movement came to a slow halt while she still felt his thickness inside of her with each love bite.

"Mmmmmh! Mmmmmmh! This feels so good, Trae. It's the best feeling ever now being your fiancée. I love this ring, too," she said as her body was finishing its release.

Her love spot was soaking wet on him. But he loved the feeling and was ready for more.

"You better appreciate this, because you're the only one ever to bring me to this point in my life, and I thank you for opening up to me as you did. It has allowed me to see and feel what real love is and should be—and that's you," he responded, bringing his hands up her back and caressing her with love.

"That's why I want you to think about staying here or somewhere else so we can share the world other than America. Just me and you living out our dreams and fantasies," Sarah said, never wanting to go back to America or Pennsylvania.

She wanted to spend her life and time with him—and only him.

"It sounds adventurous, and full of love and excitement. It would be a good thing to see the world with you, but we have to go back to the States because that's where my business and family is," he said.

Travon had never told her about Rosanna and their arrangement until now. She didn't get mad as he expected. She was more concerned with never going back to America and wanted him to get his son, too.

The two of them lay on the beach for another hour talking about life and their love for one another. They then made their way back to the house, where they showered and enjoyed more of each other and the night. Travon knew he had love with Sarah. There were no secrets, no lies, and no games from him. Now he thought about what she had said about traveling the world. Maybe it was a good idea, but how would he really maintain his business as he did day-to-day and make sure things were in order as he liked. He would have to figure that out later. Right now he was going to enjoy spending time and making love to his queen and true love.

## Chapter 17

The morning hour came fast. Travon was awakened by one of the island's staff, who knocked on the master bedroom door. He sat up in bed and looked to see what time it was. It was 9:00 a.m.

"Come on in!" he yelled out to the staff.

The staff came into the room with a message for him.

"Mr. Robinson, there's a business associate of yours outside stating that he has very important information for you."

Hearing this made Travon get out of bed fast. He thought there might be something wrong with his son or a family member. He rushed out of the bedroom and into his bathroom. Sarah sat up in bed worrying about her man and what was going on back in the States.

Travon walked out of the house and down to the dock to meet up with the associate that he assigned to keep an eye on Rosanna. It took time for the associate to find out who the male was at her house that day, but he did, along with more information.

Sarah was now out of bed and looking out the window down by the dock, where she saw a man talking with Travon. Travon seemed angry by his body language and facial expressions. This was not good, Sarah thought, because whatever it was might ruin their time on the island. *Something is wrong. What could it be?* she wondered. She had never heard Travon raise his voice or seen him so angry as now.

Travon instinctively turned around and saw Sarah standing there through the floor-to-ceiling glass window with her arms folded looking worried. He tried to give her a smile, but she already knew something was wrong, especially when she saw that his associate didn't leave the island. Instead, he stood by the dock by the yacht and waited as Travon made his way back into the house.

"Sarah, baby! Sarah, my love!" he called out.

She came in afraid of hearing bad news. "What's wrong, Trae?" she asked in the sweetest voice of innocence.

"I have to go back to the States," he said, sounding urgent.

"For what? Tell me what's bothering you, Trae. I've never seen you get upset like this."

He took a deep breath after realizing Sarah was not just a girlfriend, but was his soon-to-be wife.

"We have to end our trip early. I'll fill you in on what we believe is going on once we get in flight. Get the things you need. I'll give you a few minutes," he said.

She came closer and wrapped her arms around him.

"I love you; and no matter what it is going on, I'll still love you and be here for you," she said before kissing his lips and then bringing her arms around to caress his arms. "Can I shower first, babe?" she asked.

"I'll shower with you so I don't have to wait until you're done," he said, making her smile, knowing he would be showering with her.

She always desired him even when he was not in the mood. She had her ways of putting him in the mood, so they headed to the bedroom.

Within the hour, they both were ready to leave. The island staff was unaware of the unexpected departure, so as he and Sarah were preparing to leave, the male server came up to them.

"Will you be having breakfast this morning, sir?"

"I, I don't—!"

Before he could answer, his eyes made contact with Sarah's. In this moment, he felt that abruptly leaving and depriving her of a morning breakfast would be wrong and selfish.

"Yes, we have time," he said, not wanting to rob himself of the happiness which was Sarah.

"Follow me. We have your favorites already lined up."

They could smell the food cooking in the kitchen when they entered the dining room. The table was already set with a buffet-style layout with all of their favorites.

"This is food heaven here. They know us so well, it seems," Sarah said, savoring the food and the moment that she wished could last a lifetime.

The two of them talked and enjoyed each other's space and time. They also expressed their thoughts and hearts about the previous night's proposal and love-making session. All of this conversation and being in her presence made Travon temporarily forget his worries and problems back home.

"Sarah, I promise I'll make this up to you."

"I know you will. Besides, this ring and knowing I have you in my life are more than enough."

"I wish I could make your dream come true about never going back to the States and traveling the world. That would be the best happy ending to our love story."

Hearing him say this meant so much to her as she got up from the table and made her way over to him. She sat on his lap and caressed his neck with her manicured nails. He could feel the affection in her touch, which was backed by the love she truly felt in her heart. She wanted to tell him something else—a surprise—but it would have to wait, because she loved him too much to get into it now. She wanted him to deal with whatever it was back in the States, and then she would break the news to him.

"You are my world, Travon, and one day we'll run away and get married in a foreign country, settle down in the same country, learn a new language, and start a family," she said, expressing her true thoughts and emotions.

"I can't wait until that day. As long as you're happy, I will be, too," he said, ready to go back home and secure the problem.

## Chapter 18

A few hours had passed while they were in the private jet, and they were now only twenty minutes away from Harrisburg International Airport. Sarah was comfortably sleeping snuggled up next to Travon. He, too, had dosed off and gotten about an hour of sleep before he was awakened by a crazy dream, awaking only to see his fiancée looking sexy even in her sleep.

He was watching TV most of the flight in between caressing her hair and giving her kisses of love on her forehead. She was his wife-to-be and his happiness. Even watching the television was different, because every time he saw a couple, it made him think of Sarah and giving her everything she could ever ask for, including the wedding of her dreams.

As he was in thought, the pilot came over the intercom and got his attention.

"Mr. Robinson, we'll be landing in a few minutes, sir."

Sarah was awakened by the announcement. She then sat up and looked at her husband-to-be with loving eyes.

"Baby, we're here. The jet is about to land."

She could tell that something was still bothering him, so she leaned in and kissed him before saying, "Everything is going to be okay, babe," while caressing his face with love. "I'm here for you 'til the end, and I mean in every way."

Travon's associate was looking out the window as the jet started to descend, when he saw something that stood out to him.

"Travon, look out the window there," he said.

At first he didn't make out what his associate was seeing, until he noticed cars merging together and racing behind the jet as it touched down on the tarmac.

"Oh my Lord!" Sarah said, sucking in a gulp of disbelief of what was taking place.

Sirens could now be heard from the cars racing behind the jet's screeching tires as it came to a slow halt.

FBI and DEA agents surrounded the jet with their cars. They had their guns out and aimed at the jet and its exit door.

"Sarah, I love you, and no matter what, I want you to be happy with or without me," Travon said after leaning into kiss her soft lips as if for the last time.

Travon and his college buddies became successful in the beginning of their careers by moving tons of cocaine for the nephew of El Rey, who also went to college with them. They used their degrees together. Travon used his street smarts along with his book smarts, and they became rich and far more successful than the normal drug kingpin. They moved an estimated ten tons a year among the three of them from the East and West Coasts. This was also the reason he was so private. He was a mystery, well maintained, and punctual about everything that took place around him. He never told Sarah this, nor did he tell any female he had ever encountered. As far as they all knew, he was simply a successful businessman.

"What do you mean, Trae? Is there something bad going to happen to you and I don't know about it?" Sarah asked with her voice breaking when she saw him standing without responding to her. She stood up fast and embraced him. "Hold me," she begged as his hands rested on his side while feeling the end was near and the walls were closing in on him.

The thoughts of never coming back to America sounded like a real good idea right now to him.

Tears now streamed down Sarah's face. She felt the pain of what was going on and what was about to happen to him and the true love that she had unexpectedly found in him.

"I do love you, Travon. I really do love you with all of my heart," she said, crying. "Tell the pilot to take off. We can leave and never come back!"

But Sarah knew more than she had ever let on. When she made the statement of never coming back to America just now, it all started to come together to him as he briefly flashed back to the many times she said it on the island. His mind and paranoia told him that she was someone else, but his heart told him she was the love of his life.

The jet's door opened and the steps flipped down. The Federal agents didn't take long to storm into the private jet. They didn't even allow Travon to get off by himself.

"FBI. Travon Robinson, put your hands up. You're under arrest for drug trafficking, money laundering, and the RICO Act," the agent said, grabbing Travon's wrists and twisting them down so he could put the cuffs on him. "It's been over five years trying to get inside to take you down, and we finally got your ass!" the agent said before turning to the other agent. "Agent Santos, you want to do the honors?"

Rosanna stepped onto the jet wearing blue jeans and an FBI jacket with the decal on the front and back, along with her badge and credentials hanging around her neck. Her hair was pulled back and she was wearing no makeup. It really was not her thing anyway. She only dolled up for the lifestyle Travon was living. In the process, she got knocked up, which changed the FBI's plans, because she went deeper into the role she was playing by falling for him.

Rosanna set her eyes on the four-carat diamond engagement ring that Travon had bought for Sarah. Even with her being professional, her feelings had somehow lingered for him. They displayed when she saw the ring, because she never had gotten that far. She was now emotionally enraged, yet managed to force a smile across her face.

"Mr. Robinson, I hope you feel the pain emotionally just as I have after almost losing it all by falling for you and your bullshit when I came in to do a job. Agent Duvall, did you read him his rights yet?"

Travon turned to Sarah with lightening speed and looked into her eyes, feeling the ultimate betrayal. His heart in that very moment felt like it had been snatched out and thrown into a burning fire.

"Sarah, what the hell is she talking about!"

Sarah could not compose herself as tears streamed down her face. She cried hysterically because she, too, had come to do a job but had fallen madly in love with Travon. She told him everything about her—no lies and no secrets—except that she was a Federal agent from the DEA. Her job was to go in and get Rosanna out, and then find out what she could about Global Image Group, their finances, the meetings, and more. She did just that, but she had stopped reporting when her heart took over.

"Sarah, say it ain't so!" he snapped.

Rosanna looked on with some gratification when she saw him in pain.

"I told you we could have never come back here and traveled the world," she let out, her voice still broken as well as her heart.

But it was not breaking as much as Travon's heart was, from the onslaught of betrayal from both the mother of his child and the love of his life.

"I can't read him his rights. You do it!" she said.

Sarah pushed her way past everyone to exit the jet. She didn't want to be around and see him in pain and as torn up as he was. His eyes watered, but the anger he felt had him heating up and boiling inside. Travon was so angry that he seemed to zone out. He didn't hear anything else or feel anything else as they escorted him off the jet. They also cuffed his associate.

Agent Valerie Marie was standing by ready to take Travon into her undercover, tinted, candy-apple-red Porsche Cayenne truck.

"Aye, Slim, here's your guy. We'll keep our eyes on him in case his friends pop out on us," the agent said after placing Travon into the back seat of the Porsche.

Agent Marie's nickname was Slim, and the

five-foot-five African American woman was all about her job. She was driven to be the best at what she did, and she never cut corners. She would have infiltrated Travon herself as well as his close-knit organization within a year's time, because she would not have fallen for him or his smooth ways and affluent living. That in itself could be a lure to the average female, and she could not believe that her fellow agents Santos and Duvall had fallen victim to him and could have potentially compromised the DEA's and FBI's cases.

Agent Marie was a young-looking forty-two years old and would have never let herself be compromised by him or his money. This was the same thing two other agents thought when they entered into his world, but both of them had already been swept off their feet. They had fallen deeper and deeper undercover as they developed feelings that never should have arisen in the first place.

The convoy of Federal agents' cars started taking off one by one. Slim mixed in with them. Travon was in the back seat with his eyes closed. He embraced the pain and the betrayal that had set his mind and heart into overdrive. He tried to figure a way out this before it was too late, as the world he had lived in was now quickly starting to crumble around him. As he opened his eyes, through blurry vision, he could see Agent Marie looking at him through the rearview mirror. She was curious and wondered if he was crying because he got caught or because he was betrayed by two females that turned out to be Federal agents.

He was not crying in a bawling way. It was more in silence with tears flowing.

"You know the life you were living was bound to come to an end. It's a shame your heart had to be betrayed in order to get close to you so we could infiltrate your organization. We know everything, and I'm quite sure when Sarah and Rosanna come to full awareness of why they were after you, we'll learn more," she said.

Travon wiped his tears onto his shoulder since his hands were cuffed behind him.

"Slim, right?" he said, shifting his demeanor to the much more intricate and calculating Travon.

"Agent Marie to you!"

"Valerie Marie?"

"Yes, but call me Agent Marie," she insisted.

"I have a four-year-old son with Agent Santos. You know this, and imagine the pain he'll feel knowing his father and mother can no longer be in the same room, or that his father will be in jail because of his mother's deceptive behavior."

He then paused and awaited her response, because she was processing the entire approach about the child needing to see his father. But she also knew that Agent Santos might get some time away from the job or be relocated. She was sent in deep cover, and unprotected sex had led to this. It was not planned or a part of the FBI's plan.

"Do you have any children, Slim?"

"I told you to call me Agent Marie. Only my co-workers and friends call me Slim."

"I get it. Now, do you have any children? I ask because maybe you could somehow understand the pain I'm feeling."

"Yes, I have a son. Now, no further personal questions."

"Why is that?"

"Because my son is already at where you'll be going, and he has been for some time. As his mother on this side of the law, I cannot do anything for him," she said, feeling guilty as if she had let her son down.

A few minutes passed by with silence as Travon pieced things together.

"Agent Marie, I can get your son out free of whatever it is he was charged with."

Another minute passed by as she was now processing what he said while trying to figure out how he could do something like that. She also thought that he was either lying and/or crazy. Most of all, she thought about her son, who was serving twenty to forty years, with only five years in so far.

"I'm not pulling over or uncuffing you, if that's what you think. Then I would be in jail with you and my son," she said while laughing, almost as if to blow him off.

"I'm not who the FBI thinks I am. If you don't believe me, then dial this number and you'll have all of the proof you need."

When she heard this, her heart rate picked up because she felt like he wanted her to call his connect, which meant more people were going to be added to this indictment, so her by-the-book instincts kicked in. She took hold of her phone all ready to tap in the numbers.

"What's the number you want me to call?" she asked, thinking she was outsmarting him.

"2-0-2 is the area code. The number 2-7-9-8-8-3-9."

"Who should I ask for and what should I say?" she questioned

*I'm going to bring down the big fish in this organization, maybe even a cartel boss*, she thought to herself.

"It's going to be self-explanatory," he said.

She pressed the Call icon, which dialed up the number, and put the call on intercom, so she could focus on driving and so he could hear the call. The phone rang three times before an abrupt dysfunctional computer sound came over the phone as if it was tracking the caller. Then a digital female voice came over the phone: "You have been confirmed."

Agent Marie quickly hung up the phone as they pulled into the bureau headquarters. "What the hell was that?"

"You helping me."

"I didn't help you!" she snapped, feeling like he had played her just as he had played and lured Agents Santos and Duvall.

"Be open-minded! You guys are not the only ones that have resources. I do, however, appreciate your help," he said sarcastically, knowing he played her into doing what he wanted her to do.

He already knew she would do this because that's how FBI agents think. They always want more even if there is no more to have.

Agent Marie's mind raced now. She didn't want to get in trouble for making the call, especially if it came out that she had helped him in any way.

Once inside the garage area of the headquarters, the other Federal agents came over to the car to take Travon out.

"Mr. Robinson, when you see all of the charges we have on you, and probably more once Agent Duvall pulls herself together, you'll be spending the rest of your life in jail. You'll have plenty of time to think about how we took down you and your Mexican and Italian friends. Yeah, we hit all of you guys at the same time; but don't worry, it's what we do. Now it's cooperation time, and which one of you guys is going to strike a deal first?"

Travon started to laugh, which pissed off the agents even more, because his laughter made them think he knew something they didn't.

"I doubt you all even have a case. My business associates and I over at Global Image Group have no illegal ties or associates. I'm quite sure you'll discover this sooner rather than later, especially after wasting all of these man hours. Somebody is going to lose their rank here, guys, and maybe even be out of a job." He laughed. "I would hire you, but I can't trust any of you to even sweep the floor at the casino or inside my office building."

Although he was angered by Rosanna's and Sarah's betrayal, Travon knew he would prevail in the end. But this time he would have to tighten his circle up even more. They may even have to shut down for a year or two. It was certainly not like he and his associates were hurting for money. Travon made eye contact with Agent Marie and winked his eye at her. She turned and walked away, ignoring him but at the same time feeling guilty that she had done something wrong.

## Chapter 19

Travon was in the interrogation room with Agent O'Neil. He was a white man who stood six foot two with a slim build, brown hair, brown eyes, and a clean-shaven face. He came in with Agent Marie. Each of them was holding folders that contained case information and surveillance photos.

"Slim told me you tried to pull a fast one over on her with the phone thing," Agent O'Neil said as he took out photos and spread them out on the table in front of Travon. "These men in this photo are known cartel affiliates out of Juarez, Mexico," he said, pointing at a picture of Hector Guzman. "He's the brother of Jose Guzman, also known as El Rey, a very dangerous man that we have been watching 80 percent of his drug distribution into this country. This guy here, he was also connected to them somehow, but we have not figured that out yet or who the others are."

The other person he was pointing out was Ramon Guzman, the guy he met in college, who was the nephew of Jose and the son of Hector.

"Mr. Robinson, you can help yourself and your son if you cooperate enough to land these men behind bars forever. You may do a few years depending on the attorney general; however, the choice is yours to make."

"See, Slim."

"I told you, don't call me that!"

"We're kind of like friends now, Slim, since you helped me when you called up my associates."

"I didn't help you with shit," she snapped, feeling verbally violated and compromised by his actions.

Agent O'Neil looked over at Slim and then back to Travon. He wondered about the call that should have never been made in the first place, but the agent thought that she was on to something.

A knock came across the window. Travon looked over at the window and saw Rosanna and Agent Miller. Miller was a five-foot-eleven white male that had gone to Rosanna's place months back. He was the same person that his associate had taken a picture of at that time. Rosanna entered the room and allowed Agents Marie and O'Neil to step out.

"I would say I'm sorry, but I'm not," Rosanna said.

Her presence brought pain to him as he thought about his son and the love he had for him, and the fact that her position in life was going to deprive him and his son of time together.

"To be truthful, Mr. Robinson, I'm only sorry for my son, because he'll have to grow up without a father he really loves. He will have me and a male role model I choose to bring into my life around him."

Upon hearing this Travon grit his teeth. Yet at the same time, he thought about how he was going to make her pay for her betrayal and take his son back from her. Sarah's betrayal would also have to be dealt with. She gave him her body, heart, and mind, only to deceive him. Either she was that cruel, diabolical, and deceiving, or she genuinely had fallen in love with him. Either way, this was an outcome she could have prevented.

Rosanna didn't like the fact that Travon started smiling as if he still had the upper hand in his position.

"Hey, stupid, this is not funny. You're going to spend the rest of your life in jail unless you cooperate!" she snapped. "If you help us take them down, it will show me and our son how much you love him."

She tried to play on his emotions for their son. It was a low blow that he didn't expect from her. Then again, he really didn't know who she was, especially with the newfound discovery that she was a Federal agent.

"Rosanna, you of all people should know what type of person I am since I was not deceiving you. I don't have anything to say, because you don't have anything on me or my business associates.

So why are you wasting your time?" he asked, being confident yet still giving her a taunting smile that said, "I'm in control of this even with your betrayal." "Take note, Agent Santos, that I didn't lawyer up. That's what the guilty do," he explained as he leaned forward to take a drink of water from a cup that they had filled for him. "By the way, this water needs to be filtered."

"Don't worry! Where you're going, you can have plenty of this unfiltered water for the rest of your life!" Agent Miller said.

"Agent Miller, can you step out for a minute, please?" Rosanna asked.

"I don't think that's a good idea, Agent Santos," he said, knowing the gravity of their relationship and how they needed to send someone in to get her out since she was already too far gone.

"You should listen to your partner; besides, I don't have anything to say to you, Agent Santos," Travon said.

She stared him down, because she didn't like how this was going. She wished that she could get more out of him so he could cooperate and be home for his son one day. She had no plans on visiting him or allowing her son to go to the prison he was at, regardless of how much it would hurt her son.

Rosanna would have given her life for Travon

at one point when she lost herself going deep undercover. Their son pulled them close, but then time and Sarah's arrival had changed everything and shifted her focus back to the reason she was sent undercover.

"Mr. Robinson," Agent Miller said, "I want you to know before we leave this room, with all of the Intel that Agents Duvall and Santos have on you and your associates, you'll never stand a chance in court. So you have less than thirty seconds before we exit this room to make up your mind on what you want to do. Do you want to go to jail forever, or do you want to cut a deal?" Agent Miller said, looking down at his Timex watch that was given to him by his daughter on Father's Day and he wore proudly.

Travon sat across the table and smirked, which taunted Rosanna even more, as if he knew something they didn't. He did know they would not be able to hold him long, because he was not just a businessman/distributor for the cartel, he was also associated with people who were deeply rooted in higher government. This was something the agents didn't know and would not know until it was too late.

Being precious always allowed Travon to have a plan, a back-up plan, and even an out for when things went wrong like now. He wished he never had to use that number he had Slim call, but that was his ace in the hole, so to speak.

Travon didn't show his emotions now, but he was filled with anger and thoughts of betrayal that had torn his heart to pieces. Love would be the farthest thing from his mind and in life right now—and for a long time to come. Right now, the only thing on his mind was getting out of jail and getting even.

Rosanna no longer had feelings of love in her heart for him. Her mind-set was on getting even, which had allowed her to come back mentally as a Federal agent and not some cartel associate's baby mama. Sarah would really need some downtime to de-commission herself from the lifestyle that she was swept into, along with the love he had given her and the love she expressed to him. Those true emotions between the two were not faked from either side; however, the end result of taking him down was what Sarah had intended when she first met him.

The Federal supervisor directed Sarah to go into the interrogation room and give Travon his ring back. It would eventually go into evidence, but they wanted her to do this for two reasons: to make her end it physically, by giving the ring back that she had become emotionally attached to, and also to make him understand that the relationship was only about work.

When Sarah entered the room, Travon's eyes widened as he tried to figure out exactly what he was feeling. In fact, love came over him when he first saw her because she was his comfort zone. But just as quickly, hate took over him when he realized that he was in this position partially because of her.

She stood on the other side of the table and pulled off the ring from her finger. She held it in her hand and looked at it. She briefly flashed back to the moment when he asked the question most women look forward to hearing. She placed the ring down and slid it across the table close to him. Her eyes became vitreous, but for him it was too late for tears.

"I can't love you when work comes first. I'm—"

"No need for apologies. You did what you thought was right. Even if what you thought was right scarred my heart and mind for life. Keep the ring, because I have no use for it. I don't wish to see it or you again," he said as he tilted his head down.

He didn't want to look at her anymore. With his head down, she mouthed the words: "I still love you, Travon." She didn't say it aloud, because she knew audio was recording everything as were video cameras, but not from her angle. She wanted him to see her, but he didn't, so she exited the room and looked back one more time. He still had his head down. She would not be able to find another man like him. Even if it was all supposed to be work, this love thing was fate, and it came to both of them at the strangest time.

Travon was torn emotionally, but the reality of his situation was that he needed to man up, stay focused, and remember that he was his best asset. It was now time to wait for plan B to unfold. It would be a shock to the FBI and the DEA. As for Rosanna and Sarah, they would also be surprised by his next move, because everyone who betrayed him would pay.

## Chapter 20

At 7:01 a.m. the next morning, Travon and his associates were all set to be freed from Federal custody. This was news that greatly upset the FBI and the DEA after many years of compiling evidence using their inside agents Duvall and Santos. Little did Agent Marie know, but she did indeed assist in Travon's release. In fact, all of Travon's associates made the same call with the one call permitted to them. Some used the same tactics as Travon, which made the agents think they were reaching out to bigger fish in the organized drug cartel ring.

As Travon exited the Federal detention center, he saw his good employee and ex-side friend, Melissa. She gave him a look that said it all, meaning him leaving his true comfort zone of having her and the lifestyle he chose before settling down. No one could have predicted this except for the women closest to him, and they were Federal agents that had come into his life with the intent to destroy him, even if it meant emotionally, mentally, and financially.

Travon gave her a brief smile as he embraced her with a hug.

"It's a pleasure seeing you here. Thank you for showing up," Travon said before parting the hug.

"You're welcome. I figured I am one of the familiar faces you trust, if any at all right now;

besides, you are still my boss," Melissa responded with a smile, genuinely glad to see him free from the charges as well as the women whose negligent intentions had pulled him away from their rendezvous that she enjoyed.

As he was walking toward the Rolls Royce, Federal Agent Miller yelled out and followed behind him with the slew of reporters there to cover the story of the city's prominent businessman.

"It's not over, Robinson! We will get you! It's just a matter of time!"

Agent O'Neil stood back and looked dumbfounded. He wondered what had just happened to their case. All he knew was that the attorney general got a call in the middle of the night about all of these men; and just like that, they were all free to leave. It made him doubt that he and his men on the bureau were appreciated with the long hours and years they had put in on this case.

Travon turned and looked over his shoulders. He gave Agent Miller a sadistic smile that seemed to say, "You're not smart enough to catch me!"

He was right. Even more so was what Sarah and Rosanna felt would have gotten thrown out with all of the lawyers he had. That was just a little-known factor in this equation. The people with whom Travon and his college buddies dealt were not only cartel members and affiliates, but also connected with high-ranking CIA operatives that made sure their flow of cocaine could and would be distributed for financial means that fund covert opts in countries that didn't know that they were there until it was too late. These were secret missions that were not on record; they just happened. So the layers of protection these men had kept them successful.

As for the money laundering, none of their money ever went into their properties directly. They funded investors that actually worked for them by using their money to buy their properties. So on paper it was plausible that there would never be a trail they could figure out unless they were made aware of it. Even with agent Rosanna Santos being as close as she was to Travon, she would be asked to excuse herself every time things of that nature would come up, so she was never aware of them even to this day.

Agents Miller and O'Neil were also unaware that Agents Santos and Duvall were taken mysteriously from their homes through the night's quiet hours. They both vanished without a trace. Even Travon himself was unaware of their disappearing act, which may mean that they were already dead and long gone from this earth.

What would Travon think of this? Who would the FBI and the DEA blame?

"We're going to watch you non-stop, scumbag," Agent Miller said while still following Travon as the media outlets filmed it for the noon news.

"Agent Miller, I advise you to stop speaking to my client like this with your threats and harassment," Travon's lawyer said as they prepared to enter into the all-white Rolls Royce Phantom.

Melissa and Travon slid into the back as his lawyer, Jerry Caruso, slid into the front with the driver. The high-power attorney cost six figures, and he was known throughout the state as well as the legal world across the nation. The Italian-American stood six foot even. He was well tanned and clean-shaven with blue eyes, black hair cut close yet combed back, and well groomed, from the manicured nails and silk suit to the $1,000 Armani shoes that flowed with the Versace suit.

"Mr. Robinson, your business associates need you to fly out West for a necessary update to these events. The others will be there to meet you. Your private jet has been turned back over to your care, and I sent guys over first thing in the morning to make sure it had been refueled. It also had a maintenance check," Jerry updated Travon.

"Anything else you need, just make me aware of it and it's done." He then paused and went into his briefcase and took out a new iPhone X. "One more thing. Take a look at what's on this phone right here. I assume some of the meeting will be in regard to those images?" Jerry said, having already taken a glimpse at the pictures.

Travon took the phone and accessed the stored photos as well as the video. He instantly saw the images which gave him some gratification. Rosanna was duct taped at the mouth and bound by the hands. Sarah was also duct taped and secured with a gun that was pressed up against her head. A part of him still loved her and could feel the pain, seeing the one who won him over in this love thing with a gun pointed at her, and he wanted to help. But the other part of him felt satisfied that they got what was coming to them for their betrayal.

"Interesting images, Jerry. I see that when we call, our associates really do work through the night if need be," Travon said.

"It's what we do," Jerry responded before looking back at Travon. "How soon will my flight be ready to depart?"

"Now. I'll send word that you're on the way."

"Trae, would you like to get something to eat? I know you didn't eat what they had in there,"

Melissa asked as a genuine friend and employee to him.

"We can have the in-flight attendant prepare us something. The jet stays stocked and ready."

"I guess that's your way of telling me that I'm going with you?" she said with a smile on her face.

"You don't have to come. I just figured with you being here now coming to support me, it was for a reason. So why leave now?"

"I would he honored to join you in your travels. Maybe it will allow you to come back to the reality of who your real friends are," she tossed out there.

He deserved it, but her timing was crazy.

"Jerry, take this phone and delete the images."

"It's done," he said after grabbing the phone.

The cartel in connection with the CIA had tracked down Sarah and Rosanna, because they were intricate pieces that had caused all of this chaos, bringing attention to the cartel and their well-oiled machine of cocaine distribution. The CIA found the women, so the cartel sent their Los Zetas goons after them to bring them in, in the middle of the night. Surprisingly, neither woman saw this coming in their ultimate betrayal of Travon.

Travon now focused on getting out West as the Rolls Royce headed to the airport. He was also thinking about his son and where he could be.

Rosanna's mother only came to get him on the weekends whenever Travon didn't get him. He was hoping the cartel or the CIA didn't harm his son, because he would not know if the only person he loved more than Sarah came to harm.

Travon knew about the contracted Los Zetas assassins who were known in the underground world as Sicarios. When they came, they were the last thing most people saw before death. If they had done anything to his son, Travon would try his best to kill everyone around and involved. The thought alone bothered him, and he wanted to get out to the West Coast as soon as possible.

## Chapter 21

About five hours after Travon took off in his private jet with Melissa, they began their descent to Hector Guzman's 2,500 acres of land, which he owned for his horses to roam as they pleased. The land also boasted a private landing strip that was equipped with two hangers, one for him and the other for his guests. Each was capable of housing two jets.

The fifteen thousand-square-foot ranch house had all the amenities of a successful millionaire and cartel lieutenant, including indoor/outdoor pools, Jacuzzis in the master bedroom, and a chef's kitchen as well as a massive backyard. There were marble floors throughout. There was also a game room, full bar, stripper pole, and everything else that cartel members enjoyed during their downtime as well as a shooting range which they all really loved, especially when new guns arrived from the CIA.

The ranch was located on the edge of El Paso, which gave them access to Ciudad Juarez, Mexico.

Already at the ranch were Hector Guzman, Carmine Delarossa, and the CIA connect. Travon's college buddies, Byron, and his business associate, Ricardo Sanchez, were also present. El Rey himself was also there to get resolve and set an example so this would never happen again.

Travon's jet taxied in next to the others by the hanger, where Hector's security of Los Zetas met them in an all-black Denali. The doors opened and they exited as Travon came down the steps of his jet.

"What's up brother? Who is the cat? ?" the tattooed Sicario asked.

"My trusted employee," Travon said after he extended his hand to assist Melissa down the steps.

Melissa didn't know about Travon's other side, other than what the media had spoken about the previous night and this morning. Her presence was not welcome after what had taken place, but the Los Zetas goons would allow the boss to decide this. One of the Sicarios was already on the phone as he opened the door for Travon to enter.

"Boss, Travon has a girl with him," he said, holding up his finger to Travon to tell him to wait before he got into the truck. "Mira, check him."

"Tell him we don't need any new people coming into our lives right now," Hector said, not wanting Melissa to come to the ranch. She would have to stay back on the jet.

"Bro, your lady friend here can't come. She has to stay on the jet, unless you want her to entertain me and my crew," the Los Zetas member said with dark eyes that had seen many deaths.

"So you're going to make her sit out here? She's my guest," Travon said, trying to stand firm against the goons, but he didn't realize that their orders came from his boss.

"I don't care, bro. The boss said she can't come. She has to stay," the goon said again after securing his weapon and aiming it at Melissa.

Melissa now feared for her life, thinking and feeling as if she was going to die. The only time she had seen someone look this crazy was in the movies.

"Put the gun down. She'll stay on the jet. Chill, please," Travon said quickly, knowing they would not hesitate to kill her. Their jobs were simply not to let her in. El Rey or Hector would not lose any sleep if they killed her. "I'm sorry, I didn't think it was going to be like this," Travon said to Melissa. "I'll be back soon. Everything you need is inside."

He then leaned over and gave her a hug and then a kiss on her cheek. He tried to comfort her from the fear she was feeling. He then got into the truck that took him to the ranch.

Travon entered the ranch escorted by the Los Zetas Sicarios. They carried fully automatic MAC-11s, with thirty-two in the clip and one in the chamber. They were always ready to take care of business. They had Travon follow them into the house, which gave him a bad vibe about being there today. Could they be planning on removing him from the operation by way of murder? This was how they always conducted themselves over in Juarez when they tried to get a point across.

As he entered the room, he saw El Rey along with everyone else. His buddies greeted him with a brief smile that was not very promising.

"What's up, my friend?" Hector said before he added, "Sit down. We have a serious problem that needs to be taken care of."

Travon sat down briefly and flashed back to his college buddies with their not-so-happy smiles.

"We've been compromised by señor Robinson's lady friends, who we now know are Federal agents. I had a feeling about that one at your office, the assistant," he said, speaking about Rosanna.

Carmine stepped in to speak.

"We came to a solution, Hector, El Rey, and myself. It's your job to take care of any loose ends. It's our job to make sure no loose ends ever occur again. It's the way of the world and the beast," Carmine said while staring Travon in his eyes.

"Señor Robinson, you have to get rid of those two women who compromised our organization with their betrayal. It's our way of sending a message to the FBI and DEA," Hector explained to him before he continued. "It is my understanding that you have a son with Rosanna Santos, right?"

"Yes, we have a four-year-old together," Travon replied, now thinking about his son's well-being.

This was not the life he wanted for him, nor what he had seen for his future.

"Don't worry, it has been taken care of," Hector added.

Travon's heart leaped into his throat when he thought about his son being taken care of as he was just told. It felt like a thousand knives stabbing his heart all at once. He could feel the pain in his body and his mind overlap with multiple thoughts of what he wanted to do to avenge his son after he found out who brought harm to him.

"Help me understand, señor Guzman, when you say you took care of my son?"

A dark stare came from Hector's eyes while he searched Travon's body language. He would not try anything now with all the heavily armed Los Zetas members in the room.

"Your son is okay. He's in good hands awaiting to be reunited with you as soon as business is handled."

Travon made eye contact with his partners, Byron and Ricardo. Byron was in fear but spoke up.

"Trae, had you not left us out of the loop on the women you let close to you, we would have run their information and figured out who they really were," Byron explained.

"I'm organized and I run a tight ship, both business-wise and personally. These bitches could have deceived any one of us!" Travon snapped.

At the same time, his loud tone drew the attention of El Rey, who sat quietly surrounded by his goons.

"They would have been dead already, and

their bodies placed in front of the FBI and DEA buildings to show them what can happen when their attempts to infiltrate us fail." El Rey's booming voice instantly commanded everyone's attention in the room.

"Everyone, follow me," Hector ordered as he led the way with the Los Zetas goons following everyone out of the room and outside to the back of the ranch.

When they exited the house, Byron, Ricardo, and Travon were shocked and in fear when they saw Rosanna and Sarah on their knees blindfolded with six Los Zetas Sicarios standing at their sides, fully armed and ready to kill on command. Travon realized that having these women in his life was the worst thing ever for them and him; because from the looks of things, these contract killers came to do just that.

Travon's mind raced as he tried to figure out how this was all going to play out. He knew that they wanted Rosanna and Sarah dead; but after that, would he then become the target to be an example? El Rey had been known to do this back in Juarez, and he stood alongside and observed, because he was ready to get resolve. His presence alone would make that happen. He was not going back to Mexico without making someone pay for the infiltration of his organization.

Travon didn't understand why he still had the women gagged. No one would hear their screams on his 2,500-acre property. Hector knew this, so he commanded the goons to remove the gags and blindfolds.

"Oye, take that shit off their mouths. I don't care if they scream. It won't be for long!" he said, knowing they would be dead soon. "Here, give me your gun."

He then took his Glock 9 mm and checked to see if there was a round in the chamber, and there was. He then passed the gun over to Travon.

"Here, señor Robison. These are your friends. You need to take care of your business," Hector ordered.

The women could now see Travon without their blindfolds.

"Don't be stupid, bro!" the Los Zetas member said while standing off to the side of Travon with his gun aimed at him.

Travon held the gun in his grip. His heart raced, and his mind raced just as quickly. As much as he wanted to make them pay for their betrayal, he never thought he would be the one to physically bring harm to them. But he was now faced with this decision. How could he explain this to his son—that Mommy was not coming home because she was dead. In the back of his mind, that would torment him until the end of his days. This love thing had cost him so much at this point and placed him in this unwieldy position.

Both women had eyes of fear filled with tears, and each of them stared back at Travon, hoping he would not pull the trigger. They both hoped that a glimpse of love in his heart that they once shared together would make him not pull the trigger. But little did they know that even if he didn't kill them, the murderous Los Zetas came to do the job if he failed to do so. And he, too, would then be killed. All of this was because of their life of love and deception they once lived.

"Trae, you don't have to do this. Think about our love and the ring. Everything I said and felt was real," Sarah pleaded.

Rosanna looked at her and wished the Sicarios would kill her themselves. Sarah's words ate at him a little since their love could not be erased over night. As numb as he felt the day before, he didn't wish that it had to end like this.

"Papi, my son! Just don't let them hurt my love. Just make sure he's okay!" Rosanna said, not even pleading for her life.

She had done her job, but getting pregnant and having feelings for Travon just happened. Now all she cared about was her career and life. The safety of their son was most important, and he knew this and would die protecting him.

The goon came up behind Travon and placed his gun into his back. Two other Sicarios made their way over to Rosanna and Sarah and pointed their guns at each of the women.

"Enough of this love shit. That's what got you here in the first place! You kill them or we kill all of y'all!" the goon said while trying to impress El Rey with his firmness.

El Rey appreciated hearing this, because it was his way of life back home.

The heat in Travon's body started to rise as the level of tension seemed to surround him. He felt that imminent death was coming fast. He could see the look in Rosanna's eyes that displayed fear of the end. In that very moment, he flashed back to when times between them were good: the birth of their son, holidays, vacations, and more. But all of these good thoughts came to an abrupt end when he was brought back to the reality of the moment he was in when roaring back-to-back gunfire came from behind him. His heart leapt into his throat and he feared the worst. He looked around, only to see his two college buddies' heads had been ripped halfway off from the slugs that were just fired into their skulls, which killed them both instantly. Their bodies hit the ground lifeless, which left him to think about what his next move was going to be. At the same time, both Sarah and Rosanna started to scream and cry.

"Amigo, this is the life we live!" Hector said. "If we don't set examples, then people like the Feds could think they can just come and infiltrate our business. I like you, amigo, and Carmine and El Rey view you as an asset. Now prove them right! Your friends here needed to be done to influence you to take care of your business and kill these puntas for deceiving you and coming into our world," Hector explained.

Travon had to think fast. He knew that if he

didn't react now, he would be dead soon. Wherever his son was being held, he could also be killed to prevent retaliation in the future. These cartel bosses just thought like that. So Travon moved over to Rosanna and placed the gun to her head.

"Forgive me for this," he said, with his finger on the guard up against the trigger. "It's you and her or my son, and I have to keep my son alive," Travon said only milliseconds away from pulling the trigger, until a loud voice yelled out from behind him, which suddenly shifted their attention and mood.

"Hey, let's go. The Feds are here!" a Los Zetas goon shouted.

As those words boomed through the air from his mouth, three Federal helicopters appeared and rose up from the other side of the ranch. They were flying low the whole time so as not to be seen in their approach.

"Kill them all!" El Rey yelled out, before he and Hector took off running back into the house, where a custom tunnel in the basement led back to Juarez.

At that very moment, everything sped up. Travon turned quickly and fired on the goon behind him and then at the others standing next to Rosanna and Sarah. The other Los Zetas members left to protect Hector and El Rey.

The FBI and DEA all fired on the Los Zetas, and took them out one by one. From the chopper, they watched as Travon untied the women and helped them to their feet, so they didn't fire on him. Each of the women were partially thankful for the arrival of their fellow agents, but they were just as appreciative that Travon didn't rush to kill them. They knew deep down inside that he still cared for them, even with their betrayal.

"Go after that cabrón. He has our son!" Rosanna shouted in fear that her baby would be killed or held as collateral.

Travon took off and ran toward the house, only to be greeted by two slugs that slammed into the entrance door. They briefly halted his chase until he fired back with head shots that took out the goons trying to hold him off so they could escape. He made his way into the house and proceeded slowly. He didn't want to get caught off guard. While he was doing this, the Federal agents landed their choppers and secured the grounds.

As he made his way down to the basement, he could still hear gunfire erupt from the remaining Los Zetas still putting up a fight until the end.

He noticed an entrance in the basement floor that was connected to a tunnel that was four foot wide by six foot high, which gave the drug runners plenty of space to move metric tons into the United States. This tunnel was also used to send money back to Juarez. He could hear Hector and El Rey speaking Spanish with one another as they made their way through the tunnel. Then Travon heard a voice that stood out to him and sent a wave of fear through his body, almost paralyzing him.

"I want my Daddy. I don't want to go with you! No! No! I want my Daddy!" Young Jamir yelled out, not wanting to be with the strangers.

Even as a young child, Jamir could sense that something was wrong, and this alone made him afraid to go with the goon.

Travon could feel his heart pounding in his chest as he thought about the safety of his son. At the same time, he hoped that they would not bring any hard to him. He moved fast and raced through the tunnel, turning right where he heard his son's pleas to be let go. The right turn led down a straight forty-yard hallway lit with fluorescent lighting.

Hector and El Rey were gone; however, they left behind one of their Sicarios with Jamir as a distraction to keep everyone at bay, including the Feds, who would not jeopardize a child's life to get to them. Travon closed in and saw a goon with his gun to Jamir's back. Many thoughts entered his mind as just as many emotions entered his heart.

"Noooooo!" Travon yelled out, when he saw the look of malice and murder in the Los Zetas's eyes.

It was a look that he was about to kill his son. In that instant, he reacted as quickly as he possibly and took aim with his Colt 10 mm given to him by Hector. Travon didn't hesitate in squeezing off two thunderous rounds that roared through the closed-in tunnel. The first of the slugs crashed into the goon's face and marred his look on impact, ejecting chunks of his brain and skull out the other side. The second slug his him in his heart that erupted on impact and assisted with his imminent death.

Jamir jumped from the roaring of the gun, but at the same time, he took off and ran toward his father.

"Papi, Papi!" he shouted as jumped up into his arms.

Travon embraced his son with love, but also was concerned if any other goons were coming. So he placed his son down.

"Listen, Son. Papi has to go get the bad guys, okay?"

"Okay, Papi!"

"Stay right here, and I'll be back," Travon said as he left him at the end of the hall.

He knew that the only people that would enter the tunnel would be agents. Even if there was a fleeing goon, he would not be worried about the kid. Travon ran down the hallway to the end where he could go left or right, but he saw no one in sight. This was not good because Hector and El Rey had gotten away, and they would blame him for not taking out the Feds that had infiltrated their organization when he was directed to kill the two women. In El Rey's eyes, this would be deemed a sign of weakness, and no cartel embraced a weak link.

Travon rushed back toward his son and

wondered if the Feds would be there. *What would they think? How could he just walk away and get on the jet without them harassing him? What would they think about his college buddies being murdered in cold blood? Who would be responsible for this?* A part of him now came to the conclusion that he wished he would have killed the women, because now he too was a marked man, whether he was free or in jail.

When he turned the corner, he was greeted with the sight of Sarah holding his son's hand with her left hand and pointing a gun at him with her right. In that very moment, he could feel a sense of betrayal all over again as well as the pain and the emotions. He raised his gun at her; however, neither wanted to fire first or at all for that matter.

"Are we good?" Sarah asked, still holding her weapon trained on him.

"How can I answer that when you're the one that deceived me?" he asked her.

He didn't want to trust her, but he also wanted to be assured his son was going to be okay.

"I ask because not too long ago you were going to kill me and Agent Santos," she said, not believing that it had come to this, when their love was all good just a few days ago.

Her mind flashed back to the proposal. She would never be able to get that moment back if she lost him forever.

"So is this how our story ends, right here and right now? Me shooting you or you shooting me?"

he asked.

The thought alone burned deep inside of her, since she had to turn her back on the one person in the world who loved and appreciated her more than, or just as much as, her own father.

"It doesn't have to end like this!" she said, letting Jamir's hand go.

He ran to his father as she reached into her pocket and pulled out the ring.

"I couldn't give it back to them, and they couldn't make me give it back legally either, because it was a gift from you and your heart. I got suspected indefinitely, but the ring and what it means to me, to us, is worth it!"

"Bullshit!"

"Uh-oh, Papi. Bad word!" Jamir said.

"Sorry, Son!" he apologized, not wanting his son to get upset. "You think I'm going to lower my gun to have you turn on me again?"

Sarah's eyes became vitreous as her weapon began to lower and she placed it on the ground in front of her.

"Before you shoot me, let me put this ring back on so I know I died loving the man who once loved me!"

As she slid the ring on, she took her hand and wiped away her tears that would not stop falling. Her heart was breaking from the emotional pain she had caused him.

Upon seeing this, Travon could not pick up on if she was being deceitful or genuinely loving.

"If I lower my weapon, how do I know you won't deceive me again?"

"I never deceived my heart. I only left out the part that I was a Federal agent. When I fell in love with you, it changed everything. I stopped reporting back. I didn't want anything to compromise our life and love together. Yes, I should have told you once we started getting serious, but I'm telling you the truth now. Either accept my truth and love or just kill me; because, otherwise, I'll be dead emotionally to this world anyway."

A part of him conceded to her words that were backed by true emotions. Everything she had said to him was the truth. He would now have to lower his guard just enough to filter through everything she had said from that point on.

He lowered his gun and looked into her tear-filled eyes, and he saw what he believed was the truth and love. He just didn't want to regret what was to come, if anything else occurred between them.

He started to walk toward her with his son in tow. Sarah saw him approach and could feel her heart flutter with love and happiness. She embraced the fact that he was willing to forgive her, so they could start on a new path. He came up and wrapped his loose hand around her, and she fell into his welcoming embrace and felt his love.

"I love you, Trae! I really do!" she said, with all

of her heart and body.

"I really loved what I thought we had," Travon said, getting her attention as he slid his face across hers almost in an intimate way.

He then moved over to her soft lips and kissed her with love, hate, and passion all at the same time. He then pulled back from the kiss and looked into her eyes.

"But this will never work!"

Before she could process what he meant or had just said, he fired off a round into her side, which punctured her lungs and immediately took her breath, forcing her eyes to widen in fear of what was next. However, the pain she felt in her heart because of the love she genuinely had for him was way worse than the slug burning her flesh.

Travon still held on to her, looked into her eyes, and watched as she struggled to breathe as blood started filling her lungs and replacing the oxygen she required.

"I gave you all the love I could give you in this world. I'll see you on the other side," he said as she took her last breath.

He then laid her down on the ground. He felt as if a weight had been lifted from him, knowing that she could never betray him or anyone else again.

Jamir didn't really know what was going on, other than that his father had laid her down. In his mind, she was tired and ready to go to sleep. It was sad but far from the truth that he would never know.

Travon turned his head and looked down the hallway toward Mexico. He knew he could run that way and live a life on the run with his son. He would also make Hector and El Rey aware that he had taken care of business. However, unbeknownst to Travon, at this point, the cartel bosses could care less. He would be murdered as soon as he showed his face in Juarez.

"Mama!" Jamir called out, which shifted Travon's attention forward, where he saw Agent Santos alone with her weapon drawn on him.

She looked down and saw Agent Duvall lying there not moving. She assumed she was dead.

"What the hell happened down here?" she asked, having the drop on him.

"They got to her. They tried getting to our son, but I took out the one down there," he explained.

"I don't care about him. His body looks to be far enough in the tunnel to be on the Mexico side; but her, this is still US soil."

"You said that as if you want to line me up with this since you couldn't get me on anything else!"

"I just want all of this to be over, and that means us, too. You're going to jail, and I'll raise my son the way he's supposed to be raised."

When Travon heard what she had to say, it made him push out all the feelings he ever had for her. He didn't want to kill her in front of their child, but the fire he was feeling inside his body and the thoughts he had over her ultimate betrayal, brought him back to the reality of the situation they were currently in.

"I'm going to be a part of my son's life, whether you like it or not. Ain't that right, Son?"

"Yes, Papi! Can we go now, I'm hungry."

"Come to Mama, Son," Rosanna said.

"I can't let that happen. You want me gone. I'll go, but I'm not going to jail. More importantly, my son is coming with me," he explained as he turned around and held his son's hand in his left and his gun in his right as he brought it around to the front.

"You are not going to take my son away from me!" Rosanna yelled out, not wanting to fire on him in front of their child. But she came close to doing so. "Stop! I swear, punta, you take another step and I'll shoot you dead!"

Her words shot through the air and pained him even more, knowing that he had to do what was in his best interest. The gun was still in his hand. He peeked under his left arm and squeezed off three thunderous rounds back to back as he glanced over his shoulder and saw her face. He knew she was about to fire on him. To her surprise, she caught slugs in the face and body that twisted her around, leaving her to die. The slug to her face hit her cheek bone and went through the other side of her face. The other two slugs crashed into her stomach and chest, hitting her in the lung. Jamir strangely didn't turn around to see this, maybe in fear that something was going to happen. Travon took a deep breath and exhaled before he continued on.

As he made his way through the tunnel, he grabbed the Los Zetas goon's gun, just in case he needed it. At the same time, he took his cell phone and called up Melissa. She was so scared after hearing all the gunfire on the ranch that she answered on the first ring when she saw that it was Travon calling.

"Tell me you're okay!" she asked when she answered the phone.

"I'm good, but there has been a change of plans. I had to escape through the tunnels leading into Juarez, Mexico."

"You want me to have the pilot fly over there?"

"First, let me ensure mine and my son's safety before I have you come to this place," he said as he made his way toward the daylight at the end of the tunnel. "I'll call you back within five to ten minutes."

"Please call me back! I need to know that you're okay and what I need to do for you," Melissa said, frightened of how things had unfolded thus far.

He hung up the phone and left her to her thoughts as he made his way out of the tunnel. He saw buildings and cars, but few pedestrians other than a few elders walking around. His Spanish was not that good, but he could speak enough to get by. He continued walking with the gun tucked into his shirt now.

Once Travon had made it past the buildings, he could see on the other side of the border, through a tall fence that separated the two countries, where the ranch stood. He could also see his private jet among the others by the hanger. He had to figure out something, and fast, because he was now in El Rey's country, and his presence alone would warrant these elders to make a call to him.

## Chapter 22

Within the hour, Travon was on his jet back to Pennsylvania, thanks to Melissa's fast thinking and call to one of Travon's business associates from Global Image Group. Travon had real investors other than Hector Guzman in Mexico who didn't hesitate to pick up him and his son. They took him to the airport where his private jet landed for a quick pick-up. Thanks to having a lucrative amount of money and working with crooked officials, Travon was also never flagged for illegally entering and then leaving another country with the proper credentials.

Jamir was sound asleep looking cute and innocent to his father, who felt guilty for the life he had imposed on his son over the last twenty-four hours. Melissa stared out the window in between checking her phone for incoming calls that would need to be addressed.

Travon was still thinking about having to kill Sarah when only forty-eight hours prior, she was the love of his life. She was the one he would kill for—not kill. As for Rosanna, the scorn that she felt for him after leaving her to be with Sarah was too strong. Besides, he also discovered that she was a Federal agent. His relationship with Sarah ripped out her heart, and she wanted him to pay at any cost. Unfortunately, that cost led to her demise and being scorned until the very end.

Travon could still see Sarah's crying eyes at the moment he pulled the trigger. He knew she genuinely loved him, but he could not risk her waking up one day and turning on him and his heart again.

Now with all this behind him for now, he would have to come up with a plan C, since the CIA's assistance was plan B, which was already called in to get him and the other associates out of jail.

Thoughts of Ricardo and Byron also lingered in his head, because he knew that their wives and children would soon discover their demise. Travon would make sure that they all would be taken care of, no matter what. As for explaining what had taken place, he figured he would leave that to the FBI and DEA. He couldn't bear explaining it to their wives and children, who he knew quite well. Besides, he couldn't even say he was there.

In the middle of his thoughts, Melissa's cell phone sounded off. She looked down and saw that it was Travon's attorney calling.

"Jerry's calling. You want me to answer?" she asked.

Travon figured that Jerry Caruso had been made aware of what had taken place either by the media outlets, Hector, or El Rey, who was connected to the CIA. Trying to evade them would make the world a lot smaller if they wanted him dead, he thought. So he had to be smarter and think ahead.

"Answer it and see what he has to say."

"Hello, this is Melissa speaking," she said in a soft yet professional tone.

"Melissa, Jerry Caruso is here. What's going on?" he asked, trying to keep it brief to see what she had to say.

"I don't understand the question?"

"You're a smart girl. What happened out there?"

"I stayed on the jet. Would you like to speak to Mr. Robinson?" she asked, looking on at Travon to see if he was ready to take the call. He extended his hand.

"Put him on the line already," Jerry said impatiently.

"Jerry, how are you doing, my friend?"

"I'm great over here, but I just got a call from our friends out West and down below there. They didn't sound too happy."

"I don't know why. I secured everything they wanted me to take care of. Maybe not at their speed, but it's done. Send them that message and let them know if they want proof to check underground," he replied, referring to the tunnel.

"Yeah, I'm getting that, but you know them guys down there want one thing and the big guys here want another. The thing is, we need to talk about this when you make your way back over here," Jerry said, not knowing they were in flight back to Pennsylvania.

"I'll see you as soon as I get into town," Travon explained before hanging up the phone and realizing that he could not make it out of the meeting with Jerry. He, too, was connected with the cartel and in deep with the CIA, which alerted Travon.

After the call, Travon glanced over at his sleeping son. He knew he could not let them take him away from his boy. He would have to do what was best for him, which meant he had to prevail by surviving what they had in store for him.

"Melissa, I'm going to have to make a power move by selling all of my things I own personally as well as the things I own with my college associates. I'll let you know what businesses to keep afloat and which ones to sell. I want all my homes sold. And for your troubles, you can keep the Forest Hills house."

"I assume with all of this taking place you no longer want to stay in Harrisburg or Pennsylvania?"

"Correct. I have to think about my son and his best interests. So while you're at it, I need you to withdraw a total of $2 million from different company accounts. I'll need that in cash by this time tomorrow. I'll get two phones, one that you only use when speaking to me. When it rings, you'll know it's important and business needs to be conducted," Travon said, with his mind racing to execute his plan to the fullest.

He knew the cartel and their assistants with the CIA would come for him fast and unexpectedly.

"I know you love him," Melissa said, pointing at

the sleeping Jamir. “But if you’re running, he shouldn’t have to live that life. A child needs stability.”

“In case you haven’t noticed, Melissa, all he has is me right now. I can’t send him to his grandmom’s, since they know about that place.”

“They don’t know about me. As for the house in Forest Hills, I’ll sell it and relocate just as you did. I could move somewhere far and quiet where he’ll fit in with the other kids. Then when you’re ready to come back around, I’ll be awaiting your call. If you like, you can call every day to speak with him.”

“Let me think about it. Because between me and his mother, the only person we ever left him with was his grandmother,” Travon said as he closed his eyes and thought about his plan C and how it really needed to unfold.

## Chapter 23

Close to a year had passed since everything in Travon's world had turned around and forced him to a life always looking over his shoulder. It was not from the FBI or the DEA this time; instead, he tried to stay hidden from El Rey and his cartel goons as well as his CIA associates that deemed Travon a liability because of his infiltration by Agents Santos and Duvall. El Rey and Hector Guzman were aware that he had killed the Federal agents; however, the FBI and DEA thought that El Rey's men were responsible for this, since there were so many Los Zetas members found dead in the tunnel.

Melissa did as Travon had asked and sold all of his properties, only to funnel the money into accounts he had set up in different names or overseas accounts. He had done this just in case he ever needed to abort the plans he currently had to remain low-key.

Melissa also found herself a place in North Dakota close to the Canadian border, which gave her and Travon access to flee if necessary. As planned, she took Jamir while Travon evaded the men who were constantly searching for him. As for her being in this location, no one would expect for him to ever come that way. Over the last year, Travon had found himself trusting Melissa as a loyal ex-employee and good friend. They did have intimate encounters, but nothing with strong feelings attached other than her having his best interests in mind and him looking out for her financially for taking care of his son. Without question, he appreciated her for her support. Little Jamir was now five years old and had grown to embrace her presence, especially the way she spoiled him and gave him the world afforded to her by Travon when he was not around.

Travon had been gone for a month this time, since the last time he had stayed at her place. She bought a home with twenty acres, which gave her space and privacy for when Travon did come back. This also allowed her to get horses for the three of them.

Melissa was in the kitchen making homemade chocolate chip cookies with Jamir when her cell phone only used by Travon began to ring.

"That's my dad!" Jamir called out, since he also knew the phone on which he called.

"Yes, it is your dad, little man!" she said as she wiped the cookie dough from her fingers before answering the phone. "Hello, stranger!"

"How's everything going with you and my boy?"

"We're doing fine, and he's in chocolate chip cookie heaven right now, because that's what we're making."

Travon laughed a little, knowing that they were his son's favorite treat.

"Don't let him eat too many. I don't want to

spoil his dinner," he said.

When he made that comment, Melissa knew that he was near.

"I guess I should set the table for three?"

"That sounds good to me."

"I have something special to fill you in on, too. I think it'll bring some happiness back into your life," she said.

"You know I'm not big on secrets or surprises."

"It's not a secret or a surprise," she said.

As she was talking, there was a knock at the front door followed by the doorbell ringing.

"Hold on, Trae. Someone's at the door."

She made her way to the front door and looked through the peephole, but no one was there. She looked through the living room window, but didn't see anyone standing on her porch. There was also no sign of a car driving away.

"I don't know who it was, but there's no one out there," she said after getting a bit suspicious.

She then made her way back into the kitchen with Jamir. When she walked in, she was shocked and surprised when she saw Travon sitting there with his son. He was eating one of the burnt chocolate chip cookies from the first batch she tried to make.

"Don't ever scare me like that, mister! I don't like surprises!" Melissa said with her hand over her heart, which was still racing.

Jamir sat there with his father. He was happy and smiling while chewing away at the burnt cookies.

"I told you to always make sure the doors were locked."

"Normally, they are, but I burnt the first batch of cookies, so I had the door open. Then when I closed it, I forgot to lock it back up," she responded as she walked over to him and gave him a kiss on the cheek and then on his soft lips.

This kiss was a welcoming sign that allowed him to know he was at home. Home is really where the heart is. However, he would not let her know how he really felt anytime soon to prevent from getting hurt again. He would simply enjoy her space and time, just as she would with him.

"So what is the surprise you have to tell me?" he asked, after kissing her warm and welcoming lips one more time.

Little Jamir started pointing toward her belly.

"I'm going to be a big brother," he said in between chomping down on his cookie.

"He's right, I'm pregnant. I'm three months in so far!" she said with a smile in her eyes and on her face.

She lit up when sharing the good news with Travon. At the same time, he also felt good knowing that he would always protect her and his expanding family.

"So I'm having another son?"

"Really? I don't even know yet!"

"I want a brother, so we can play together," Jamir said full of joy and innocence.

Travon smiled because he, too, wanted a boy; however, if he had a girl, he would spoil her just as much.

"I really appreciate you, Melissa. Words mean little when there are more actions and emotions being expressed. I just wish this was the path I had chosen in the beginning instead of looking the other way when I had a jewel—a treasure—in you all of this time." Her eyes still smiled just as much as her heart. She leaned in and kissed him once more.

"I appreciate you and what we have, too. What's understood doesn't need to be explained," she said while caressing his neck. "We're going to be a family. I have you and Jamir's best interests at all times. There's no second-guessing that. Plus, with the baby I'm having, what more could I ask for?"

## Chapter 24

Four months had passed now, with Travon successfully evading the cartel and their associates. There had not been any close calls or signs of them looking for him either. As for his son, Jamir, he was growing in all of his young innocence while waiting to be a big brother. He talked to Melissa's pregnant belly every day and rubbed it as well. Travon was also excited about having another baby boy to join his son. At seven months and one week, Melissa was ready to bring her baby boy into the world so she could be even more of a family with Travon.

The time that Travon and Melissa had shared up until this point had only allowed their physical and emotional bond to grow even more. He now used the word and words he never thought he would ever say to a woman again. She embraced it each time, knowing how significant it was as well as what it meant when those words flowed from his heart through his mouth.

"Melissa, baby, I'm going out for a run while you and Jamir go shopping for baby clothes. Don't let him pick out all the clothes like you did last week. He likes what he would wear, not what the baby should be wearing," Travon reminded her while rubbing her belly and kissing her soft, warm lips. "I love you, pretty lady!" he said, which always made her feel sexy, even during her pregnant months when most women don't feel attractive.

Travon was well aware of this, but he felt that his woman was very sexy with her pregnant glow.

"I love you, too, Trae. I love this thing that got me knocked up, too," she said while caressing his manhood.

"Now, do you really want me to go jogging with a hard-on?" he said, which made her laugh.

He was not erect, but it got a laugh out of her when she put the visual with his words.

"I'll be gone roughly an hour, so I'll probably be back before you."

"If my feet start hurting while walking around, I'll try to keep up with Jamir in the stores, but then we'll come back early. Don't worry, I got this," she said after giving him one more kiss before he left for his run.

She gathered up a few things, and then she and Jamir headed out to the car and off to the mall to shop for the baby.

As they both left the house, somebody was watching them exit and go their separate ways. At the same time, this person made a call to his boss to let him know of their new find, meaning Travon and his little lady friend.

"I found our old friend."

"Are you sure?"

"I'm 100 percent sure! It's him, his son, and this new girl he's with who's pregnant."

"I guess we'll pay him a visit then," the voice on the other end of the phone said.

Travon didn't see someone lurking in the brush since he blended in with the landscape. If he had, he would have never left his woman and child alone, nor would he have taken off running to clear his head and stay in shape.

A little over an hour had passed by as Travon was finishing up on his run and closing in on his place. He took notice of a few vehicles on his property: two black Range Rovers and an all-white Mercedes Benz G500 truck. They were all parked side by side by side. He didn't recognize any of the vehicles as being owned by anyone he had met and lived in the area, which caused immediate alarm as he picked up his pace and also saw Melissa's red Toyota Avalon parked at the house. That meant she had come back early from her shopping trip, and it also meant that she and his son were inside the house with people he didn't know.

He ran over to his Chrysler 300 C Hemi edition with the V8 engine, custom black paint, tinted windows, and black rims. He opened the door and went into a compartment that held his twin Glock 9 mms and took them out. They were already ready to roll and loaded with sixteen in the clips and one in the chamber.

Travon entered the house through the garage to give himself the advantage of surprise. Once he was inside, he passed through the laundry room and then into the kitchen. He could feel his body temperature rise with each step. At the same time, his heart raced as fast as his mind. He tried to figure out who these men were, and more importantly, where they were in the house with Melissa and Jamir.

As he made it further into the house, he could hear voices speaking Spanish with one another. This was not good! *Hector or El Rey has found me!* he thought. The love he felt for his son and Melissa was making his heart feel pain; however, his precocious mind was processing the situation. He closed in on the voices and walked into the living room. Before entering, he stopped, took a deep breath, and exhaled as he swung around with his guns in front.

That was when he saw Melissa lying on the floor saturated in blood, with his son at her side, lying his head on her and rubbing her belly. There were two men standing over her, with four of them standing next to Hector Guzman. The two standing by her caught the barrage of slugs that instantly killed the two of them. He then shifted toward the men by Hector, killing three of them and wounding the other as Hector ran toward the door to escape. But not before Travon fired multiple shots in his direction slowing him down as they slammed into his back, legs, and shoulders and taking him down abruptly. At the same time, Travon raced over to the one downed yet still moving Los Zetas and fired off a shot into his face, which killed him instantly. He then made his way back over to Hector.

"You come into my home with my family and bring them harm!" he snapped as he pulled the trigger again to no avail.

Both of his weapons were empty. Hector then started to laugh through his pain to taunt Travon.

"Faggot! You kill me, and my family will kill everyone connected to your bloodline!"

A smirk formed on Hector's face, which sent even more pain streaming through Travon's body as he briefly glanced over his shoulder and saw his son still rubbing Melissa's belly and telling her she was going to be okay.

Travon snapped both mentally and emotionally after having to witness the woman he loved down and looking to be dead. Without bullets left in his guns, Travon began crashing their butts into Hector's head and face, over and over again. He vented his anger and pain that was taking over his body, heart, and mind.

Hector grunted as Travon continued slamming the butts of the guns into his face to display his pain. His swollen eyes spewed blood from the gashes and lacerations that came from the blunt force.

"Papi, she needs your help!" Jamir called out as Melissa moaned and moved a little.

He stopped in mid-slam of the butt of the gun and made his way over to Melissa. He took her phone from her pocket and called 9-1-1.

"9-1-1, what's your emergency?"

"My woman has been shot, and she's pregnant! I need help. My baby needs help," he let out with his voice broken and shaken all at the same time.

"The baby's moving, Papi!" Jamir said, with his hand still on Melissa's belly.

When Travon heard his son say this, it made him choke up even more. The baby was moving inside of her because of all the blood she was losing and from the trauma of being shot.

Travon relayed his address to the dispatcher before hanging up, even though the operator wanted him to stay on the line a bit longer.

"Melissa, baby, I'm here. Don't leave me. Look into my eyes, baby. I love you!" he pleaded with all of his heart and love for her.

At the same time, he hoped to God that his unborn child would be fine.

"You are all going to die!" Hector yelled out, beaten and battered. "You can't hide from mi familia," he said, with a smirk through his marred face. "You let those Federal bitches take us all down. You'll never have a full night's sleep with El Rey and his goons looking for you!"

Travon stood up from Melissa's side and walked over to one of the dead Los Zetas members. He then grabbed his gun and walked over to Hector.

"You will never see the day that I or my family meets their demise. And just like you, El Rey won't see me coming," Travon warned as he fired off a round into Hector's face, killing him instantly, before he tossed the gun onto his lifeless body.

Sirens could be heard fast approaching as Travon made his way back over to Melissa, with hopes they would arrive in time to save her and the baby from the trauma she had gone through.

Travon held her head up and looked into her eyes. He could hear the police and paramedics closing in on the house.

"I love you, Melissa. Stay with me, baby. Please, stay with me!" he said, all choked up.

Her eyes opened and looked into his, and a smile formed on her face.

"I, I, I love you, too, Travon!" she said before closing her eyes as her body went limp.

In this moment, holding her in his arms, he felt like the life had just left her body.

"Noooo! Melissa, baby! Open your eyes! Please open your eyes!" he pleaded as the medics rushed into the room and over to assist her.

"Sir, we're going to need you to step back. What's her name?"

"Melissa!"

"How far along is she with the baby?"

"A little over seven months. Please save her!"

"My baby brother's in there," Jamir said, pointing at her stomach as another medic took him away, since he thought the boy might be injured as well with so much blood on him.

They quickly began CPR and tended to Melissa's gunshot wounds. They knew they needed to race back to the hospital for a more stable environment.

"Sir, we're going to need to ask you some questions about all of this," the police officer said after seeing the dead bodies lying around the room.

"I have to go to the hospital with my son and lady," he said with his eyes locked on them as they were taken through the front door.

"These men came into my home where my seven-month-pregnant woman was with my five-year-old son. You see all this? I was defending my home," Travon said, walking out and making his way to his car to follow the ambulance to the hospital.

The police officer didn't follow him because he knew Travon would come back to his home due to the type of situation this was. He also knew he would go to the hospital and not leave his son or his woman who was pregnant with his child.

Further questions could wait; besides, it was self-explanatory for the most part.

## Chapter 25

Six months later and Travon, Melissa, Jamir, and Michael were all at their new home in the Ohio suburbs with new identities. They were a bit unnecessary, however, since El Rey had been killed by an up-and-coming cartel boss. No one was looking for Travon anymore, even though he remained cautious and protective over his newborn baby, Jamir, and future wife-to-be Melissa, who had been bound to a wheelchair after being paralyzed from the gunshots which had struck her spine.

Without question, Travon could live with this decision, because he truly loved her whether she could walk or not. "I didn't fall in love with your legs," he would say to her when she questioned if he still loved her. He would let her know that he loved her even more now with their son and being a family.

Today they were sitting on the back patio of their new home that boasted one hundred acres with an in-ground pool, playground, go carts, and horses in the stable. Melissa was holding baby Michael and feeding him. Travon jumped in and out of the pool with Jamir. She really appreciated the view of the man she had fallen in love with and who loved her no matter what.

"Hey, sexy lady. You want to come over here and join me in the water?" Travon asked.

"Don't you see me breast-feeding our baby boy?"

"After you're done, join us and have some fun," he said before picking up Jamir and throwing him into the air.

Jamir loved it as he splashed down into the water, before coming back up and swimming over to the edge of the pool. He then climbed out and walked over to his baby brother and gave him a kiss on the cheek.

"I'll teach you how to swim when you grow up, Michael," he said before he turned back and ran toward the pool to jump in and splash his dad.

Melissa still had a smile on her face. She loved what she was seeing in her man and stepson.

As she sat there breastfeeding, a feeling came over her that made her excited.

*This can't be happening!* she thought.

"Oh my God! Trae, come here!" she yelled out.

He climbed out of the pool and made his way over to her. Jamir also got out of the pool and stood beside his father, mirroring his movement.

"What's going on?" he asked.

"Look at my feet!" she said while sitting in her wheelchair.

He looked down and saw her wiggle her toes, which was something the doctors didn't expect to happen anytime soon. Travon saw this and became hopeful, just as she did.

"Your little piggies are moving!" Jamir said as he extended his little fingers to tickle her feet.

She started to laugh when she felt the sensation.

"Stop, Jamir, before you make me drop your baby brother," she laughed.

"God is good. He works in mysterious ways," Travon said, leaning in to kiss her lips and make her heart feel the love and appreciation of her presence. "I love you and your little piggies as Jamir called them," he said, which made her laugh.

"You're so stupid, you know that?" she said with a smile, moving her feet even more. At the same time, she started to feel her legs again, as if there was a pinched nerve that had been unblocked. "I can feel my legs, too, Trae!" she said before becoming emotional.

"Give the little man a feeding break. I'll hold him. Use your upper body strength to see if you can stand," he said, taking his son in his arms.

She did just as he had asked her, and she tried to stand up. She struggled to her feet and fell back into the chair. She then looked up at him only to try again. This time she made it to her feet as the remaining sensation in her feet and legs came back slowly. She could not believe it as tears of joy slid down her face. Jamir came in close and hugged her leg, sending innocent affection into her body along with the love that she saw in Travon's eyes.

"For better or for worse, you didn't give up on me or our love," she said with her legs shaking but still standing.

"This is what we both have been looking for all our lives. Why leave when times get hard if love is still there? Believe it or not, we have always been in God's plans to come together and be one. We just had to go through this process," he said as he leaned in and kissed her, which made her feel complete as a woman. "Loving you is only going to get better from here."

"Now you can marry my daddy," Jamir said, adding his thoughts on what should take place next.

Melissa's heart filled with love when she heard her stepson say the words all women look forward to hearing. The look in her eyes said the rest. The love in his eyes spoke volume. What more is there to say when you find someone you love and appreciate this much?

***To order books, please fill out the order form below:***
***To order films please go to www.good2gofilms.com***

Name: ____________________________________________
Address: ____________________________________________
City: ______________ State: ______ Zip Code: ______________
Phone: ____________________________________________
Email: ____________________________________________
Method of Payment: Check VISA MASTERCARD
Credit Card#: ____________________________________________
Name as it appears on card: ____________________________________________
Signature: ____________________________________________

| Item Name | Price | Qty | Amount |
|---|---|---|---|
| 48 Hours to Die – Silk White | $14.99 | | |
| A Hustler's Dream - Ernest Morris | $14.99 | | |
| A Hustler's Dream 2 - Ernest Morris | $14.99 | | |
| A Thug's Devotion – J. L. Rose and J. M. McMillon | $14.99 | | |
| All Eyes on Tommy Gunz – Warren Holloway | $14.99 | | |
| Black Reign – Ernest Morris | $14.99 | | |
| Bloody Mayhem Down South – Trayvon Jackson | $14.99 | | |
| Bloody Mayhem Down South 2 – Trayvon Jackson | $14.99 | | |
| Business Is Business – Silk White | $14.99 | | |
| Business Is Business 2 – Silk White | $14.99 | | |
| Business Is Business 3 – Silk White | $14.99 | | |
| Cash In Cash Out – Assa Raymond Baker | $14.99 | | |
| Cash In Cash Out 2 - Assa Raymond Baker | $14.99 | | |
| Childhood Sweethearts – Jacob Spears | $14.99 | | |
| Childhood Sweethearts 2 – Jacob Spears | $14.99 | | |
| Childhood Sweethearts 3 - Jacob Spears | $14.99 | | |
| Childhood Sweethearts 4 - Jacob Spears | $14.99 | | |
| Connected To The Plug – Dwan Marquis Williams | $14.99 | | |
| Connected To The Plug 2 – Dwan Marquis Williams | $14.99 | | |
| Connected To The Plug 3 – Dwan Williams | $14.99 | | |
| Cost of Betrayal – W.C. Holloway | $14.99 | | |
| Cost of Betrayal 2 – W.C. Holloway | $14.99 | | |
| Deadly Reunion – Ernest Morris | $14.99 | | |
| Dream's Life – Assa Raymond Baker | $14.99 | | |
| Flipping Numbers – Ernest Morris | $14.99 | | |

| | | | |
|---|---|---|---|
| Flipping Numbers 2 – Ernest Morris | $14.99 | | |
| He Loves Me, He Loves You Not - Mychea | $14.99 | | |
| He Loves Me, He Loves You Not 2 - Mychea | $14.99 | | |
| He Loves Me, He Loves You Not 3 - Mychea | $14.99 | | |
| He Loves Me, He Loves You Not 4 – Mychea | $14.99 | | |
| He Loves Me, He Loves You Not 5 – Mychea | $14.99 | | |
| Killing Signs – Ernest Morris | $14.99 | | |
| Kings of the Block – Dwan Willams | $14.99 | | |
| Kings of the Block 2 – Dwan Willams | $14.99 | | |
| Lord of My Land – Jay Morrison | $14.99 | | |
| Lost and Turned Out – Ernest Morris | $14.99 | | |
| Love & Dedication – W.C. Holloway | $14.99 | | |
| Love Hates Violence – De'Wayne Maris | $14.99 | | |
| Love Hates Violence 2 – De'Wayne Maris | $14.99 | | |
| Love Hates Violence 3 – De'Wayne Maris | $14.99 | | |
| Love Hates Violence 4 – De'Wayne Maris | $14.99 | | |
| Married To Da Streets – Silk White | $14.99 | | |
| M.E.R.C. - Make Every Rep Count Health and Fitness | $14.99 | | |
| Mercenary In Love – J.L. Rose & J.L. Turner | $14.99 | | |
| Money Make Me Cum – Ernest Morris | $14.99 | | |
| My Besties – Asia Hill | $14.99 | | |
| My Besties 2 – Asia Hill | $14.99 | | |
| My Besties 3 – Asia Hill | $14.99 | | |
| My Besties 4 – Asia Hill | $14.99 | | |
| My Boyfriend's Wife - Mychea | $14.99 | | |
| My Boyfriend's Wife 2 – Mychea | $14.99 | | |
| My Brothers Envy – J. L. Rose | $14.99 | | |
| My Brothers Envy 2 – J. L. Rose | $14.99 | | |
| Naughty Housewives – Ernest Morris | $14.99 | | |
| Naughty Housewives 2 – Ernest Morris | $14.99 | | |
| Naughty Housewives 3 – Ernest Morris | $14.99 | | |
| Naughty Housewives 4 – Ernest Morris | $14.99 | | |
| Never Be The Same – Silk White | $14.99 | | |

| | | | |
|---|---|---|---|
| Shades of Revenge – Assa Raymond Baker | $14.99 | | |
| Slumped – Jason Brent | $14.99 | | |
| Someone's Gonna Get It – Mychea | $14.99 | | |
| Stranded – Silk White | $14.99 | | |
| Supreme & Justice – Ernest Morris | $14.99 | | |
| Supreme & Justice 2 – Ernest Morris | $14.99 | | |
| Supreme & Justice 3 – Ernest Morris | $14.99 | | |
| Tears of a Hustler - Silk White | $14.99 | | |
| Tears of a Hustler 2 - Silk White | $14.99 | | |
| Tears of a Hustler 3 - Silk White | $14.99 | | |
| Tears of a Hustler 4- Silk White | $14.99 | | |
| Tears of a Hustler 5 – Silk White | $14.99 | | |
| Tears of a Hustler 6 – Silk White | $14.99 | | |
| The Last Love Letter – Warren Holloway | $14.99 | | |
| The Last Love Letter 2 – Warren Holloway | $14.99 | | |
| The Panty Ripper - Reality Way | $14.99 | | |
| The Panty Ripper 3 – Reality Way | $14.99 | | |
| The Solution – Jay Morrison | $14.99 | | |
| The Teflon Queen – Silk White | $14.99 | | |
| The Teflon Queen 2 – Silk White | $14.99 | | |
| The Teflon Queen 3 – Silk White | $14.99 | | |
| The Teflon Queen 4 – Silk White | $14.99 | | |
| The Teflon Queen 5 – Silk White | $14.99 | | |
| The Teflon Queen 6 - Silk White | $14.99 | | |
| The Vacation – Silk White | $14.99 | | |
| Tied To A Boss - J.L. Rose | $14.99 | | |
| Tied To A Boss 2 - J.L. Rose | $14.99 | | |
| Tied To A Boss 3 - J.L. Rose | $14.99 | | |
| Tied To A Boss 4 - J.L. Rose | $14.99 | | |
| Tied To A Boss 5 - J.L. Rose | $14.99 | | |
| Time Is Money - Silk White | $14.99 | | |
| Tomorrow's Not Promised – Robert Torres | $14.99 | | |
| Tomorrow's Not Promised 2 – Robert Torres | $14.99 | | |

| | | | |
|---|---|---|---|
| Two Mask One Heart – Jacob Spears and Trayvon Jackson | $14.99 | | |
| Two Mask One Heart 2 – Jacob Spears and Trayvon Jackson | $14.99 | | |
| Two Mask One Heart 3 – Jacob Spears and Trayvon Jackson | $14.99 | | |
| Wrong Place Wrong Time – Silk White | $14.99 | | |
| Young Goonz – Reality Way | $14.99 | | |
| | | | |
| Subtotal: | | | |
| Tax: | | | |
| Shipping (Free) U.S. Media Mail: | | | |
| Total: | | | |

**Make Checks Payable To: Good2Go Publishing, 7311 W Glass Lane, Laveen, AZ 85339**